Smoky Ordinary

Stories by Kathy Flann

Winner of the Serena McDonald Kennedy Award

Snake~Nation~Press
Valdosta, Georgia
2008

Acknowledgments

I thank all of my teachers—Jim Clark, Lee Zacharias, Fred Chappell, and Rod Smith. I thank Michael Parker for many years of guidance and support. Judy Troy has been invaluable, not only for her knowledge of craft, but for her kindness and encouragement—without it I would have been lost many times. I thank all of my readers—Julianna Baggott, Alan Bissett, Lucy Collins, Lisa Day, Matt Ellsworth, George Green, and Tita Ramirez. Thanks to Didier Simon for opening his home in France to me for several months while I was redrafting this book. I thank my family—Dad, Kate, Stephanie, Rachelle, Homer—for their love and support. Thanks to my mother, not just for her encouragement, but also for her amazing cover art.

Publication Credits

"Experiments": *The North American Review*

"Missing Person": *Yemassee*

"Permanent Resident": *Shenandoah*

"A Happy, Safe Thing": *Shenandoah* and *New Stories from the South*

"Strike Anywhere": *Quarterly West*

"Indian Summer": *The O. Henry Festival Stories*

"Black Lagoon": *Crazyhorse*

"Profile of the Addict": *The Texas Review*

"Mad Dog": *White Eagle Coffee Store Press*

"An Airtight Box": *The Del Sol Review*

"The Dispossession of Billy Montgomery"
first published as "El Corazon" in *The Barcelona Review*

The Price Campbell Foundation
Barbara Passmore

ISBN 978-0-9754843-8-8

Table of Contents

About Kathy Flann

Kathy Flann earned an MA with a Creative Writing Concentration from Auburn University and an MFA in Creative Writing from UNC-Greensboro, where she served as Fiction Editor of *The Greensboro Review*. She has taught Creative Writing at several universities in the US and England. During her five years in the UK, she served on the board of directors of The National Association of Writers in Education. Her novella, *Mad Dog*, which appears in this collection and which addresses the ex-patriate experience, won the AE Coppard Prize for Long Fiction.

Cover Art by Karen Flann

"Spiritual color veiling", taught by Barbara Thelin Preston, was the beginning of Karen Flann's art journey. After exploring watercolor and abstract acrylic painting with a series of nationally recognized teachers, she became fascinated with abstract collage. As a result, she has become something of a bag lady, constantly looking for stray bits of material to be incorporated into her next piece of work.

Currently she is a member of the Springfield Art Guild, the Vienna Arts Society, and the Fairfax Council of the Arts. Recently, she held her first one-woman show at a local library. Her work has been accepted into numerous juried shows and is held in many private collections. In addition to the art for this jacket, she also created the cover for Kathy Flann's novella, *Mad Dog*. It was her great joy to collaborate with the author to create the cover of this wonderful collection of short fiction.

About the cover

Collage with rice paper and found materials. Since my recent work is abstract collage, it was a departure to do something more representational. In addition to the fun of creating the cover, it was a wonderful surprise when the barber appeared in the barber shop.

Photography by Dan Coyle

Daniel Coyle, a semi-professional photographer for the past 15 years, lives in Washington, DC but spends his weekends traveling the back roads of Maryland and Virginia in search of arresting images of rural and small-town life. His work has been shown in galleries in Tempe, Arizona; Raleigh, North Carolina; and Berkeley Springs, West Virginia.

Dedicated to my brother, Robby, 1969-1984

Judge's Statement

Kathy Flann's story collection, *Smoky Ordinary,* has a wonderful affinity with Sherwood Anderson's *Winesburg, Ohio* in its keen-eyed and compassionate chronicling of an out-of-the way American place and the people who populate it. The main difference between the two books, other than the passage of almost a hundred years, is that Flann gives us a late twentieth century/early twenty-first century update on the lives of American citizens in their daily adventures and the anxieties and hopes that accompany those adventures. But the common artistic denominator, which remains between the two books, is expressed perfectly in Sherwood Anderson's dedication of *Winesburg, Ohio* to his mother, who, "taught me to see beneath the surface of lives."

This penetrating vision is Kathy Flann's primary strength as a fiction writer and her gift to her readers: seeing beneath the surface of her characters' lives and doing so with both courage and empathy. What most enables her to illuminate *Smoky Ordinary's* intriguing underbelly is her virtuosity with narrative voice and point of view. Her versatility as a storyteller gives her the access she needs to animate and reveal human experience in this social outpost on the Atlantic seaboard. Her wit, her flare for creative detail, and her ability to dramatize a story with an exceptional sense of conflict and tension provide her with everything she needs to take us deep inside the fictional universe she has named *Smoky Ordinary.*

Kathy Flann's accomplishment here is noteworthy on both local and global scales. The stories grip, hold, and reveal on individual planes of meaning while contributing to the integrity of the social and cultural perspective of the collection as a whole. She knows and loves this world in spite of its drawbacks and disappointments. Anyone willing to enter it with her will be richly rewarded.

Brian Bedard
Vermillion, South Dakota
October, 2007

Brian Bedard is a Professor of English at the University of South Dakota where he directs the Creative Writing Program and serves as Editor of the *South Dakota Review.* His short stories have appeared in a wide variety of magazines, and his new collection, *Grieving on the Run* was published in 2007 by Snake Nation Press.

Smoky Ordinary

Stories by Kathy Flann

Winner of the Serena McDonald Kennedy Award

Snake~Nation~Press
Valdosta, Georgia
Founded 1989

A Happy, Safe Thing

My older sister, Minnie, and her new husband, Sax Smithers, whom she met six months ago, are going to show up half an hour late for their wedding reception. They get held up on the way to the American Legion because all six guys from the pharmacy, where Sax sorts boxes of pills, want a ride, right then, in front of Shepherd of the Hills Methodist Church, in Grandma Tillie's brand new 1983 Cadillac convertible. Then, Minnie, excited not just about the wedding, but also about her graduation from Smoky Ordinary High School yesterday, smuggles me into the passenger seat, ignoring what Mom and my stepdad Frank and Grandma Tillie have said over and over about my heart.

"Okay, Sheryl," Minnie tells me. "Slouch down in the seat, and nobody'll know." Minnie's best friend, Gina Potts, is in the driver's seat. On the front steps of the church, Frank is hugging the pastor again, and Mom, who's still in the doorway, is too weepy to see us. Minnie, behind me, pinches my cheek and then snuggles up to Sax as if leaning forward from their back seat perch to talk to me has kept her away from him for too long. Sax smiles with his eyes closed.

My heart brought Minnie and Sax together; it's how they met in the first place. My heart is built backwards with a hole in the middle. The pharmacy where Sax works and where I pick up my heart medication after school on Wednesdays is next to J.E.B. Stuart Jr. High; I just finished the seventh grade there. My stepdad Frank makes Minnie pick up my medication sometimes, when I'm too tired, and that's how Sax recognized her and felt all right talking to her that "destined" (as Minnie says) Sunday morning at P&W's Eatery, where Minnie waits tables. Now, she always says to Grandma Tillie, who wanted Minnie to study court stenography at the community college, "See Grandma T? You can make your future anyplace. I started making mine December 30, 1982, at a restaurant on Coover Street."

About my heart: It keeps me from riding in airplanes because the air is too thin, and Mom, Frank, and Grandma Tillie keep me from riding in convertibles, too—or pickup trucks or hayrides—because Mom says it's not good for me when the air rushes past and makes me catch my breath. My heart also keeps me from running, biking, or swimming, but I can walk far enough and can play badminton in the backyard. I can beat all comers at badminton.

Dr. Brooster, our cardiologist up at Fairfax Hospital, says mine is a best-case scenario. He says one in five thousand kids have a heart like mine, and so far, at thirteen, I've outlived all the others like me. After we saw Dr. Brooster in April, I sat in the hall watching a bright-blue fish in the aquarium try to push a smaller yellow fish out of some thick plants—as if the plants were going to hurt him, I thought, as if the blue fish were the mother and the yellow fish the child. I overheard Mom say to Dr. Brooster, "How long? Five years? Ten years?" And he said, "She's doing fine." And then I heard Mom say, "Maybe you just don't want me to know."

I tried to stare at the aquarium when Mom came out of Dr. Brooster's office. But I saw her mouth tight and worried. When she looked at me, we both put on happier faces.

Now, as we drive out of our way on the bridge over Lake Iroquois, Gina Potts honks the horn while Minnie and Sax yell and hoot, holding each other tightly. I look from the gravel spitting off the tires to my sister and Sax. They had their first kiss in a rowboat on the lake, and now I watch them steal another kiss in the back of the Cadillac, Minnie's veil blowing over both their faces. On the other side of the bridge, the town disappears into Virginia forest, pine and oak trees thick as cotton. Just as it seems we're on our way to Haymarket, the next town over, Gina turns us around. As we drive the last eight blocks toward the American Legion, the dark sky, gloomy since the morning rain, makes the town look brighter, especially Pink's Tiny Pink Grocery and the orange Phillips 76 sign and the hands of well-wishers waving in the gray afternoon.

We pull into the circular driveway and coast to a stop in front of the Legion Hall, which Minnie used to call "the soldier palace," where Mom and her two friends from Tuesday night Apostle Bingo at Redeemer Baptist are busy on the big side lawn getting ready for the reception. They have moved almost everything from under the big white and yellow striped tent she rented and into the building, because the sagging middle of the tent, heavy with water from the early morning downpour, is leaking into a family-sized fried chicken bucket.

Minnie told me she has pictured her wedding reception on the nicely mowed Legion lawn ever since Frank started taking all of us to his first

Vietnam Veterans socials there five years ago. From way back then, she pictured a pastel tent and herself waltzing in a white dress with a long train. I don't think she counted on the sky being dense and ugly and the lawn swarming with gnats. But today she has Sax and the white dress and the train, and she doesn't seem to notice anything else.

After we get out of the car and walk up the brick path to the side lawn, she does notice that Mom's hands are shaking. Mom's seen me in the convertible, and we stare at Mom together for the few seconds she pretends to ignore us. She bustles under the yellow tent, the sleeves of her pink suit hiked up, revealing arms tender and pale as a baby's. Then she can't take it any more and comes our way.

"I hope that was worth the two years you took off your sister's life," she says to Minnie, and turns right around again, angrier and shakier than even the time Minnie lost Grandma Tillie's locket. All her excitement from this morning and over at the church is gone. Mom covers the potato salad quickly, pouncing on it with Saran Wrap as if it's wild and doesn't want to be touched. Then, she jabs her finger in the middle of the lemon meringue pie and puts a gob of meringue in her mouth. She closes her eyes, her jaw muscles moving. When she opens them, she looks across the big lawn and across Jefferson Street and across the town square and past the statue of Stonewall Jackson—all the way, it seems, to the clotheslines along-side Betty's Azalea Ranch, where I can just make out a housecoat hanging next to a pair of overalls. "Well, never mind," she says finally. "It's a special day and you want to do special things. I know that." She brightens then, swats at the gnats hovering over the cheese plate, and looks at us. "I know that," she says, and smiles like we all share a secret.

Mom paid a lot for the tent. Two weeks before the wedding, over in Haymarket, five miles east of Smoky Ordinary, Buy or Rent quoted us a price of two hundred dollars. On the way home Mom said, "Two hundred dollars?" She leaned closer to me and half-whispered, "I only decided to go along with this wedding because, well, they were going to go to the Poconos and do it without us if I didn't. But, as far as I'm concerned, they're too young."

"Sax'll be twenty next month," I'd muttered. Mom popped a Certs in her mouth and stuffed the wrapper in the ashtray. Her eyes were as wide open as she could make them—I imagined them rolling on the floor of the car like brown and white marbles. It's what she does when she gets frustrated, which isn't very often; she's known for being one of the happier people in Smoky Ordinary.

"Mom," I'd said, "I think the wedding theme should be hearts. We'll buy little napkins with hearts on them and have heart-shaped balloons in nets on the ceiling that we make fall down during the first dance. We can have heart cake four layers high and hearts on the tablecloths." Mom's eyes returned to their normal size and she looked over at me. "I can be the expert decorator," I said, and she smiled for real, with teeth showing. She started to say how nice that was, and I pulled from my wallet the card the doctor gave me—a picture of a healthy heart on one side and a picture of a heart like mine on the other. "My card?" I said, handing it to her just as I had seen Frank do with important customers at the lumberyard he manages. I like playing the ham.

"That's in bad taste, honey," she said, looking at me as if I'd become someone else's daughter, only she seemed sadder than she'd be with a stranger.

"I wanted to cheer you up," I told her. "I didn't mean what you think." But she didn't talk to me again the rest of the way home.

Minnie, who has no idea the trouble Mom went to for the tent, now heads toward the building with Sax and Gina on either side like attendants to a big, white parade float. Mom mops her forehead with a little heart napkin (they were Valentine's Day leftovers on clearance, the only heart thing we ended up getting) and puts her other hand on her hip.

"Well, we're almost done," she says, partly to me and partly to her two Bingo friends, who are making trip after trip into the building. They nod and smile and say, "Thank God" and "Whooey." Mom doesn't like Apostle Bingo, but she goes because, she says, Grandma Tillie wants to and Grandma Tillie shouldn't drive at night by herself, especially not in a brand-new car without a ding in it. Besides that, Mom says, there are a few nice people there who aren't holy rollers.

"Honey," Mom says, "you can handle these, can't you?" and she hands me a bag of Kost Kutter dinner rolls. "And why don't you check on Grandma Tillie while you're inside? She looked dizzy to me. Or maybe like her legs were tired." Mom always says that between Grandma Tillie's hypertension and her blood clots, a stroke won't need a fancy invitation. So, Grandma Tillie only sweeps or pulls up weeds when Mom isn't around because even Grandma doesn't like Mom's wide-eyed look, which she says is like a basset hound in the rain.

"Okay," I say, taking the rolls, "see you inside," and I walk into the building, which is red brick and has white pillars and the words "American Legion" and "With Liberty and Justice for All" attached to the front.

The letters are made of stone and there's a bird's nest in the "u" in "Justice." Inside, off to the left at one end of the long room there is a stage with an American flag backdrop. The DJ Frank hired stands on stage playing Foreigner's "Urgent" and thumbing through the rest of his records. He's squinting through his reading glasses. The opposite wall is covered with maroon draperies and in front of them are twenty card tables with chairs. A long buffet table and a small table with the wedding cake on it separate the card table area from the rest of the room, which is empty. Guests chat under the shadows of antlered heads—deer, elk, moose, caribou—along the side walls. Frank says the animals are arranged so that if they had bodies, they would be standing in formation.

After I take the rolls to the table, I stand towards one corner of the room, wondering when something's going to happen. Hardly anybody's paying attention to the bride and groom, and nobody's even dancing. I guess I'm not the only one nervous—Grandma Tillie, sounding a little angry, tells the DJ to change the song and goes and gets Sax to be her partner. The two of them dance right in the middle of the big empty part of the room, and the guests standing under the animal heads along the side walls either whisper and stare or pretend not to notice. The DJ hasn't changed the music, but Grandma Tillie is getting funky, waving her index fingers, and she won't stop for anything, not even Frank, who tries to cut in and get Sax back to Minnie.

"This old lady's still got something left," Grandma Tillie says, and Frank waves his hand as if to say, "Okay, you win." Minnie, Gina Potts, and two other girls have sat down in folding chairs around one of the card tables in the back of the room. I hear them worrying that no one else is going to dance.

"It's those heads," Gina says. "They're gross." Minnie keeps peeking at Sax, who's winking at her and good-naturedly swaying while Grandma Tillie revives the Charleston. Minnie sneaks looks out of the corners of her eyes as if no one will notice she's doing it. "Minnie," one of the girls says when they all notice she has stopped listening. Minnie looks at them and smiles and blushes like she's been caught sucking her thumb. I go back over to the buffet table and open the bag of rolls, put them on a Chinette paper plate and set them next to the cheese.

"That's a lot of food," a voice says behind me. I turn to find Eddie Strubinski, the only guest my age. He lives next door to us in a pale green house. Frank calls it "the tall foxhole" because both the house and the sickly green grass in front of it are the color of camouflage. Frank says the people that painted the house are probably the same ones who put the animal heads in formation, people who talk about the war like it was fun because they weren't really in it.

"Hope you're hungry," I say to Eddie. Before we left for the church this morning we heard Eddie's mother, Lucille (of House of Lucille Beauty-Care Salon), yelling that Eddie would eat his eggs and grits and like it.

Eddie is wearing a blue suit jacket and a tie, but his long brown hair is tucked behind his ears like always and he's still got on the same pants he wears to school every day, brown corduroy with frayed bottoms and a POW-MIA patch on one knee. His father went to Vietnam when Eddie was three and disappeared, but Frank says there's no evidence that he disappeared in Vietnam; he probably disappeared in Atlantic City or Miami or who knows where. Frank says that some guys, even one in his own unit, just don't want to go home. Eddie says his dad's probably in a little cage living off bugs and rain water. I point at his pants. "Nice of you to wash them for the occasion."

"My mom made me," he says and looks embarrassed. He usually says "shut up" when people, especially his mother, mention his pants, and I suddenly feel bad.

I don't know why I said it unless it's because I'm angry, not at Eddie, but at Mom's happiness being covered up with worries about Grandma Tillie and me, about whether we're dying or whether we're living enough. And I think I'm also being rude because I know I can be. Eddie once sent a paper airplane note into my window that said "Sheryl" on it, and there were stars around my name. "Sorry, Eddie," I say, both about his having to wash his pants and about me talking about them.

Eddie doesn't answer me; he's loading up a plate with miniature hot dogs, and so I watch Minnie, at the card table, whispering to Gina Potts. And right then, maybe because of the light shining from her wedding ring when she cups her hand to Gina's ear, I realize that Minnie will be gone from our house forever. Tonight when I go to bed, I won't hear her over on her side of the bedroom, winding her carousel music box in the dark and listening to it play "Evergreen" with that tiny plink, plink sound until she falls asleep.

Either chastened by Grandma Tillie or bored, the DJ stops the record and announces that the lovebirds will now cut the cake. Everyone should gather around the cake table. Minnie rushes past us, holding her train with both hands. Eddie and I try to hand out plastic forks to people as they hurry over for a good view. Sax presides over the gathering from behind the cake, looking like he might be responsible for the announcement. "I just wanted to get my baby back," I hear him say.

Frank, in front of the cake, begins to make a speech, something he does whenever more than five people gather at the American Legion Hall. Mom likes this trait; she says "Frank opens up," which is something our father never did. He left before Minnie started school and I was a baby. "Sheryl," Mom says, "if I had a nickel for every time I've missed your father, I'd be a poor woman." Frank clears his throat to get everyone's attention.

"Listen up, folks," he begins, like we're his platoon. "Thank you all for coming," he adds, softening his tone. "What can you say about a day like this? We are lucky to share it with family and friends. Some people don't have what we have—a home, food on the table, four intact limbs. But, most importantly, some people don't have love. And what have you got if you don't have that? You've got diddley squat. There's plenty of love in this room tonight. Most of it's coming from right behind me."

Frank turns around, and, as if they've practiced it ten times, Minnie and Sax push cake into each other's faces and everybody laughs. Several ladies squeal. Then Sax kisses Minnie and, after a minute, dips her, and suddenly it's as if they've forgotten the rest of us are here. Sax has one hand around her waist and one in the middle of her back, and she looks like she's not holding herself up at all. Their faces are as peaceful as happy sleepers.

Watching them, I'm not thinking about my empty bedroom anymore. I first try to imagine what a real kiss would feel like, and then wonder how they forget that another person's saliva is being rubbed on their mouths. But a second later, I think I know how they forget. I even wish I knew what Sax's lips felt like, and I start to imagine, like I sometimes do, that I'm kissing Cooper Matthews, a boy from my art class who has tan legs and light brown hair and gets paint on his nice face when he concentrates on what he's seeing in his mind and twirls his brush. Then, I quickly look down at the forks in my hand, afraid someone might see what I'm thinking. I stare at the frayed bottoms of Eddie's pants, which are rustling as he rests on one foot and then the other.

"For Pete's sake, do you think this is some kind of peep show?" Grandma Tillie shouts, and Minnie and Sax come up for air with everybody laughing. Grandma Tillie looks proud of her joke, though a little surprised that it turned out to be one. Eddie's mom, Lucille, pushes through the crowd, making her way toward where Eddie and I stand, and Eddie says quickly, "We're out of here," using the same lieutenant tone of voice that Frank had a minute ago. Eddie takes my arm and rushes me toward the side door that opens onto the lawn and the leaky tent. He flings the door open even though it says, "Use only in emergency." When I look over my shoulder, Lucille is hugging a woman and patting the woman's tall hair as if it's a dog.

"Eddie," I say, "I don't think she's looking for you." But he keeps pushing me along and we go outside.

As the door shuts slowly by itself, I hear Mom, inside, laughing, and I wonder what Minnie or Grandma Tillie or Frank are doing to change her mood. Eddie lets go of me and paces under the tent like he might run away any minute. I lean against the building and try to catch my breath.

"Don't you like weddings?" I say.

"I like funerals better," he says and then looks shy all of a sudden and turns his face away. "Like at my grandfather's funeral," he tells the trunk of the dogwood tree next to the tent, "everybody got up and told great stories about him."

"But he was dead. Why is that better?" I say, and Eddie turns and pokes at a red cooler my mother has left on top of the table.

"It's not better exactly. But like, with your sister and her husband," he says, pointing at the Legion Hall, "you don't know what's going to happen. You don't know where they'll end up living, or whether they'll have children, or if they'll see the children grow up. You don't even know if they'll be happy."

"But that means their lives could be full of surprises," I say.

"Or not." He stares at the palm of his left hand. "Bad things happen. You just don't know when."

The wind has picked up and blown ripe green leaves onto the table. Eddie and I do not talk for a moment, and the wind whistles under the tent. Eddie's dark brown hair blows into his eyes and he moves it away with his hand; he opens the red cooler.

"Pay dirt," he says and pulls out a bottle of Andre pink champagne.

"Go ahead and drink it," I say. "Mom must have forgotten about it."

Eddie pops the bottle open like he knows what he's doing and takes a long drink even as it's foaming out off his wrist and down his arm, turning his coat sleeve dark. His face looks how I feel when I ride on the handlebars of Minnie's bike—like he's a free agent and nobody's going to tell him to eat his eggs and grits.

"Here, you have some," he says. He hands me the bottle and I find myself reaching out to take it. Dr. Brooster has said to me, "As you get older, Sheryl, kids will be drinking. But you can't. Say it with me now, 'I can't drink.'"

"I can't drink," I say to Eddie.

"I knew that. I should have known that. Sorry." Eddie sets the champagne bottle, half empty now, back on the table.

"Let's go back in," I say. When I turn toward the door, Eddie takes my hand and stops me.

"Sheryl?" he says. And as I turn toward him again, he kisses me. He has his eyes closed and his hair spills onto my face. When I close my own eyes, I notice that Eddie's lips don't feel the way I imagine Cooper Matthews's—warm and full and golden tan. Eddie's lips feel like Eddie—thin and pale and trembling. And they touch mine in a way I never thought of, like he's saying all of the things he couldn't fit on a paper airplane note. When we stop kissing, he puts his hand on the side of my face as if he's wanted to for a long time.

"Are you mad?" he says.

"No. I liked it," I tell him, and I have a strange feeling of dread, like maybe I'm telling the truth. Eddie takes his hand away and moves his hair from his face the same as he always does, with his small, pale hand and thin fingers, his nubby fingernails, but now it almost hurts me to see him do it. Because all of a sudden, it's like his hand holds me inside it. And suddenly, I understand that love isn't the way I thought—it's not a small, happy, safe thing. It's like rain; it keeps falling whether you need it or not.

"We should go back in," I tell him, but I don't move toward the door, and this makes him smile. I listen to the sound of leaves moving in the wind, and Eddie rocks back and forth on his feet, his hands stuffed deep in his pockets, and his happy face looking up. I look up, too. The sky, almost black now that night is closer, seems closer, too, with its swirling clouds and its glowing spot where the shrouded moon is rising.

Inside, the lights have dimmed and nearly everyone is dancing, and the hall doesn't feel empty anymore. Lucille finds us; she tells Eddie she wants him to see a plaque on the wall that lists his father as a soldier missing in action.

"I'll be right back," Eddie says to me, and as they walk away, I hear Lucille tell Eddie that the plaque had shone out at her like an angel, like a sign from above. "I've been in here before," she says. "I don't know how I've never seen it."

The small disco ball Gina Potts had tacked to the ceiling is making tiny white lights move slowly over the guests like snow. Mom and Frank are doing the twist to Journey's "Separate Ways," Mom's hands hanging limp from the wrist and her hair coming loose in curls around her face.

Flann

I see Grandma Tillie standing next to the buffet table, and when I go over to her she puts her arm around me and we watch the dancing. Minnie and Sax, in the middle of the crowd, are the only people slow dancing. Minnie has her arms around Sax's neck, and he has his hands on her waist. They sway slowly, and Sax stops to gather up her train, which has spilled onto the floor and gotten caught under her heel. He holds it up for her when they start dancing again.

"Do you think they'll always be this happy?" I say to Grandma Tillie.

"Oh, honey," Grandma Tillie says. "Sometimes they'll be much happier than this."

Profile of the Addict

Everett believes a normal person is someone who thinks about things instead of doing them. Like thinks about leaving pictures of himself under the windshield wipers of his ex-wife's car. Or thinks about sitting up all night in a lawn chair in her driveway. Or passing notes, via his six-year-old daughter, that say: "I'll forgive the whole thing if you make that guy move out." Everett believes a normal guy wouldn't actually do those things.

Because of his job in visitors' reception at the Smoky Ordinary Town Hall Jail, he has to carry a gun, which, although he's never felt especially comfortable around guns, is not so much a problem in itself. However, now it is one in the morning, and he is standing in his ex-wife's front yard and he is still wearing the gun. Normally, he would have removed it the moment he clocked off, would have stowed it in its case and placed it on the top shelf of his locker. He has never forgotten before, not in ten years. But he looks down, and there it is. And now he is a guy lurking outside his ex-wife's house with a loaded weapon.

Yet he can't bring himself to leave. He can't even make himself move, get the gun off his body, stuff it under the blankets in his trunk. He wants to keep watch over the little brick bungalow where he so recently lived. He wants to stay and study the drawn curtains, to picture his wife and daughter sleeping in their respective rooms. He knows What's His Face is in there somewhere, but it doesn't matter, because he knows where Joy and Crystal are—together in the house. And his water balloon of a heart begins to swell, bulging with hope in his chest, as it does each night when he stands here. One day soon, Joy will see her mistake.

And yet his library book, *Profile of the Addict*, says, "Where there is addiction there are lies." When the other security officers at the Smoky Ordinary Town Hall Jail say to him, "How's it going, Everett?" he says, "Can't complain." Though it isn't true, because he could. He could complain because he's had insomnia, because he's been aching with weariness, either outside Joy's house or at his apartment flipping though

13

pictures of their honeymoon in Biloxi or making construction paper cats to mail to his daughter, Crystal, who's six and loves cats. And he could also complain because he hates his job, hates the proximal pain he feels buzzing in mothers to visit their sons in jail, sitting in that glass booth shuffling through paperwork, telling people which of their loved ones are going to be released and which aren't. Your son? I'm sorry, sir, but the judge says he needs your wife's signature. . . . Sir, it's not my problem that your wife has disappeared again. I need her signature or else the kid stays. His job is largely to keep people apart.

And they're people with no money. He sees people, lots of people, with eyes swollen from the drugs they take or used to take, and they're the reason he picked up the book. Everett's buddy, Mickey, who's also a guard, says they do it because they're selfish. They'd rather get high than get a job and take care of their kids. The book, however, says addiction results from vulnerabilities in the ego and self-structure: "Wherever there are psychological vulnerabilities, individuals develop characteristic traits which attempt to compensate for, even as they reveal or betray, those vulnerabilities." What saddens Everett about these people is that they compensate by leaving the earth, shooting up, their eyelids drooping so they can't see anything of hard, messy reality.

But then again, is that so different from what he's doing now? The fact that he forgot to leave his gun at work betrays something about him, about his inability to accept his fate.

He takes a deep breath and then exhales, his head lolling back so he can study the summer constellations and listen to the night. The tree frogs and crickets are singing. Paul Wynn, another insomniac, who lives next door, sits in his study hammering out "The Sting" on piano, and his little dachshund howls in the background. Traffic on Route 66, a half a mile away, whooshes in the distance like the ocean.

Everett glances at the gun again. Maybe it's okay. He is less a threat than a bodyguard or something.

But then, as he is thinking about this, his index finger gets all tingly, like it does after he's been at the shooting range. He can sense the safety and the trigger at his hip, almost like they are hot and alive. What if something happens in his brain, the synapses misfire, and he draws the gun from the holster? What if he points it at her window? His hand hovers at his side and it is so light, like it isn't his, isn't attached to him. What if there is some part of him, even just a small part, that wants to believe it would be easier if she didn't exist? Panic rolls through the whole length of his body, icy cold, and he gasps.

He runs down the block to where he has left the car, gets his flashlight from the glove compartment, and rummages under the front seat for the book.

It's not only the addicts he encounters through his work; Everett's father's drug had been cocaine. In days past, it was exotic, something hard to find just a few miles out of Washington, DC. But his father hauled freight all up and down the seaboard, and in all those cities one could locate just about anything. Eventually he drove off and left twelve-year-old Everett and his mother behind. His mother saved her hairdresser tips for a year to run a *Have You Seen This Man?* ad in a New York City newspaper. Still today, twenty-three years later, she keeps her husband's clothes in a box in her closet, as if he might turn up for a change of shirts, as if they might pick up where they left off, never arguing, but making careful requests. Would you mind if I slept on the sofa? It's me. I'm just feeling a little . . . I don't know. In their marriage, it was like they mistook politeness for respect. And Everett's mother thinks the abandonment was just some misunderstanding, because surely he wouldn't have been rude on purpose.

Everett doesn't drink alcohol, or even coffee, but a part of him has been waiting all his life for addiction to catch him, as if it is inevitable like death. He flips the book open and, as is his habit, skims through the pages, looking for a passage that will speak to him, help him regain control. His buddy Mickey tells him his only problem is that he spends too much time at the library. "If you want to boink that red-haired librarian with the limp, just go over and talk to her. You don't have to read everything in the whole place." But it isn't like that. Now, his eyes following his index finger, he reads through a section on symptoms, even though he has read this section three times today: obsessive behavior, denial of reality, weight loss, listlessness, a tendency to lie to oneself and others.

His breath pinches his throat when he turns to another section, one he hasn't read before. "Addiction is a fatal illness," it says. "The person usually dies from behaviors that result from the addiction rather than from the addiction itself." He puts the gun in the glove compartment, underneath the car manual, and slams the door shut.

In the morning, Everett takes sick leave from work. At the bank, he withdraws all of the money from his savings account. He comes home briefly to safety-check his apartment. He tests the smoke detector and unplugs appliances, so he won't be responsible for setting the neighbors on fire. He leaves a phone message for his wife and Crystal: "Hi. If this is Joy, I want to tell you I'm gone to Drakewood Center—you know, that place over in Brilliant. Call you soon." He takes a bag of perishable food out to the garbage, wheels the bin to the curb, locks up, and heads over to Brilliant in his old Honda. He drives past his cousin Pink's grocery, which isn't really a grocery anymore so much as a gourmet deli; Pink wears a woolen Irish flat cap because the new suburbanites who've moved out here find it charming. He waves at Pink, who is taking some boxes to the curb; Pink smiles, puts down the boxes, and waves his cap. Then, Ned drives past the families rowing on Lake Iroquois, through the Accotink Forest, and just a quick few miles up Route 28 East, parallel to Interstate 66, cars whooshing toward DC much faster than Ned's car ambles along this old road. With the radio on and his elbow in the June sun, it's like he's about to go on a cruise. Because here, finally, he has found something he can do.

It's well-known locally that a Redskin got over a cocaine habit at Drakewood and a famous senator recovered there from exhaustion; Everett is eager to see the place itself instead of just the stately gate at the border of the property, which he has been past a million times. The building is at the top of a hill on the south side of Brilliant, a new suburb. Except when Drakewood was built twenty years ago, Brilliant didn't exist and one of the draws to the place was its absolute seclusion within miles of forest. Not anymore, that's for sure. Across the street from the gate, there's a strip mall with a giant Staples and an Applebees. Once he maneuvers through the open gate and uphill, up the twisty route, overgrown to the drive's edge with enormous tulip poplars and lichen-covered oaks and ferns and honeysuckle, he is amazed to find that the place still feels secluded. He spots the ranch-style brick building ahead. Through the trees beside him, he catches flickers of the roofs of the new Willow Landing housing development below, with their skylights and extra wide chimneys, the sort of houses Joy always wanted and that Everett has promised to build for her in a note he recently delivered via Crystal.

When he gets out of the car, he stops to take in the clean, shady air and to take a good look at how those houses have been made. Then he reminds himself that Joy has only ever written back once. It was about a month ago. Crystal had dashed from the front door of the house, the light blue envelope clutched in her hand, her face tight with the responsibility. "Here you go, Daddy," she had said, breathless as she climbed into the car for her weekend visit. He had opened it there, before they drove away. The note said, "This is the way things are, Everett. I don't know what else to say. PS I found some of your stuff in the basement.

I'll leave it on the porch for you. J" He had read it over and over, glancing up to smile at Crystal, thinking about how Joy wrote "the porch" instead of "my porch". It had seemed like she still included him in her notion of home without even knowing it. Now, though, when he thinks about it, he suspects the note just meant what it said. He suspects that because of his problem, he makes himself see things he wants to see.

Everett steps into the Center, and while the receptionist types his address and phone number into her computer, he eyeballs the brown and tan lobby with its art-deco light fixtures and paintings and its wall-to-wall carpet and walnut end tables. He thinks about how different this reception area is from the one at the jail where he works. He always sits in a little glass booth, like the one in front of him now, except that the glass is bullet proof, and the booth itself is much smaller. And the reception area he looks at all day has white plastic chairs and cinder-block walls. He imagines how much calmer people would be if the reception area looked like this one, and he thinks about talking to Mickey, his friend from work, about the prospect of redecorating. But he knows what Mickey would say: "Wall-to-wall carpet? Christ, are you kidding? Remember that drunk bastard who pissed in the corner? We'd still be smelling that shit. You'd still be smelling it, every day for eight hours."

And Everett imagines saying, "But at some point, don't you have to take a chance, believe in people?" That's what he needs from Joy, after all, just a chance. Everybody needs a chance.

He can hear Mickey again: "Hi, I'm from Earth. What planet are you from? Take a chance on some of these guys, you'll take a shiv between your ribs, too."

What's wrong with being hopeful? Everett thinks. Then he remembers how his book says that denial of reality is one of the most difficult things to treat. Maybe Mickey is right.

After Everett fills out some forms, a young man appears from the long, plush-carpeted hallway to the left of the booth. A clipboard under his arm, he shakes Everett's hand. "I'm Allen, your intake counselor," he says. "It's a pleasure." He doesn't look like Everett imagined. He isn't an older guy with a gray ponytail and glasses. Instead, he looks younger than Everett and he's freckled and wears Dockers and a golf shirt. "I've got a couple of other people I need to talk to. Someone will be along to show you to a referral room, but it might take a little while because we're kind of backed up. Just be patient and I'll meet you there as soon as I can. We'll have a chat about why you're here," he says, gesturing to the clipboard with his knuckles. "I think you'll find you've made a decision that'll truly transform your life." And then, shaking Everett's hand again, he strolls down another long hallway, to the right, leaving Everett there in the lobby.

For a moment, Everett stands at the big windows and thinks about taking off. He hasn't totally cracked up yet, and though the cost of this won't completely break him, he'll certainly feel it. And then he thinks about his life down there, beyond the suburban sprawl of Brilliant at the bottom of the hill, beyond the steadily shrinking band of woods that separates this town from Smoky Ordinary's apple-shaped water tower five miles away, and he thinks maybe his life over there is even less appealing than revealing himself to this guy who looks like Opie.

Everett parks himself and begins to wonder if he is supposed to bring his duffle bag from the car now, if they'll even let him go back out to the car once they've started their work on him, and he thinks how nobody ever tells you how you're supposed to act in the majority of situations a real person faces. It's then that he notices this other guy across from him, an older man with a salty beard and a twitchy leg, his faded leather jacket jingling. The guy has his fingers laced together across his lumpy belly and his eyes closed and he could almost be praying.

"What're we doing here?" Everett says to him. "How has it come to this?"

The guy opens his eyes, leans forward, and looks at Everett square. "Smoke?" he says and gestures to the door.

"Yeah, sure, okay," Everett says. The guy gets up and he is as tall as Everett, six feet two, except he is heavier and he walks like he's heavier, strides that would rattle the dishes.

Everett has never smoked, though he pretended he did once, thirteen years ago, so that he could meet Joy. She used to speed-walk laps around the town square in her hygienist scrubs during lunch hour. Everett lived in a basement apartment beneath Ray-Dougleman Law Offices on the square and he drove a forklift second shift at the K-Mart distribution center out by what is now the Brilliant exit on I-66. And so, not yet fully awake, he used to sit on the front stoop at noon and wait for her to walk by, her arms pumping, her blonde hair swinging back and forth on the boxy green shirt. He was twenty-four, desperately lonely, and turned on by all of the women who cut across the square to the P&W's Eatery at lunchtime, even though he'd known some of them all his life. But this one, this strange blonde one who cried and smoked while she walked—at night in bed he imagined holding onto her, and not even in a sexual way. He just wanted to hold her. Before they had spoken, he had an elemental need for her.

And so he sat on the bench by the statue of Stonewall Jackson one day and pretended to look for something in his pockets and made a show of not finding it. When Joy walked by, he waved and asked if he could get a light. She stopped and pulled a lighter from the pocket of her green pants and handed it to him. He had no cigarettes—he hadn't thought it through any farther than saying something to stop her—so he took the lighter from her and pretended to inspect it for a moment. Then he made a show of fishing in his pockets again, but slowly. He smiled at her.

"My father has emphysema from smoking," she told him. "He suffocates. There's nothing we can do."

He had one of his life's few moments of true inspiration. "Well, then, we won't smoke."

"Yeah?" she said, cocking her head, smiling. "When are we quitting?"

"Now," Everett told her. "Right now." He dropped the lighter in the trash can on the other side of the statue. He held out his hands for her cigarettes and threw them in there, too.

How many times did Everett hear Joy tell this story to her girlfriends over the years? And it always ended with: "That's when I knew Everett was the one."

The one what? he thinks now. Everett and the guy head outside, back into that cool wet shade, and they stand just beyond the entryway, with its canvas awning and its rock garden borders and its happy little fishpond. His name is Herb, and he says he's already been at Drakewood for a few days, that he is a Vietnam vet and a biker and a guy who drinks too much. He says to Everett, "I'm the sort of guy who keeps shrinks rich." Then he says nothing for a while. His face is sort of like one of those yard gnomes, stoic and pensive. It has the same eerie stillness that Everett used to sense in his neighborhood on Sunday mornings, a few years before the divorce, when all the bikes and Big Wheels just sat out there touched with dew like they were waiting for those kids to climb back on. Joy used to step into the wet grass and stare at them like they disappointed her, and she would sip her coffee and let out this big sigh. In those days, when Crystal wasn't yet sleeping through the night, and Everett's shifts at work were changing every month, there was an unnerving hush between them, in their silence an expression of their exhaustion, but something deeper, too. Lately, Everett has been

19

thinking how it's those quiet things that didn't seem awful but really were—those appear the worst when he's looking back, trying to figure out what happened. He feels like he was tricked into being happy, either by someone else or himself.

Herb packs the Marlboros against his palm, takes out two, lights one, and then passes the other cigarette and his lighter. His fingers are red and shaky like it's cold outside, but it isn't; it's ninety degrees, and there are grackles in a nearby dogwood making a godawful racket, enough to make Everett think of that movie, *The Birds*, starring Tippy Hedron, whom Joy sort of resembles. He imagines birds attacking Joy in her yard, and himself picking them off with a BB gun, and Joy being so grateful that she takes the gun and shoots her boyfriend, Larry the Professor, right in the ass. When Everett snaps to, he feels guilty for fantasizing about guns like that, even non-lethal ones. His book says there are warning signs long before somebody comes apart altogether, like the first cough on the way to pneumonia.

He closes his eyes and puffs on the cigarette. He doesn't inhale, but his heart still races. He curls his tongue and lets the smoke roll around in his mouth. The taste is bitter and sharp, but he can understand how Joy's father, Stan, grew to love it, in the same way a person could grow to love coffee or whiskey or the hard burn of cocaine. He can picture how Stan looked in the hospital when he finally died; it was a year after Everett and Joy had married. Stan was pale blue against the sheets, watery blood trickling from his nose, his body pulling in a deep desperate gasp even after he was dead. And Everett thinks about Joy clenching his hand, how he pulled her close, how she let herself be drawn in, how they were one person. Everett thinks about the possibility that he has reached the logical end of his addiction, just like Stan had his—Everett thinks how he is gasping inside, blue and nearly dead.

"So," he forces himself to say to Herb; "what brought you here? How'd you decide to do this?"

Herb pauses and looks at Everett like he's a noisy insect. It's like what Herb really wants is for someone to stand next to him and do nothing more. He wants someone to block out the emptiness and fill up some of the vacant air, which is so sickeningly vast sometimes that it makes a person want to lie down and cover his face, as if it is nerve gas, as if it can kill. That's the exact reason that at home after work Everett likes to listen to the TV as loud as he thinks the neighbors can take—and it still never seems loud enough.

Herb clears his throat, and it seems like, for a moment, he considers whether he needs to bother responding at all, but then he does. "DUIs," Herb says. "It was this or else six months in the pen." He steps away from the awning, into the rocks, and leans against the wall and glances at the treetops, at the patchy sky. "I've got the cash. So I picked this."

Everett wonders if he's telling the truth or if the shit hit the fan in some other way—he blacked out at his construction job and nearly cut off someone's leg with a jackhammer or he drove his motorcycle through the window of a doctor's office and killed a baby. "Well," Everett says, "What do you think of it?"

Herb shrugs his shoulders. "I don't know," he says, tossing the cigarette to the concrete and grinding it with the heel of his black boot. "What's your story?"

Everett tells him about Joy, about the separation, about her affair with the professor of her Family Health and Communication class at the community college.

"Well, I don't know how that qualifies you to be here, but the guys with clipboards are going to like your story," Herb says. "It's pretty ironic about that boyfriend." He smiles. "Family Health . . . ."

"Yeah," Everett sighs.

Herb pulls out another cigarette and lights it. "My counselor says every problem people ever have is caused by one thing."

"What is it?"

"Fear," Herb says. "Deep, huh?" He presses the cigarette to his lips and laughs; his hand stops shaking for a moment.

Everett thinks about Joy and about all of the incarcerated people at work. "What, like fear of being alone?"

"For you, maybe." Herb smirks and looks across the big parking lot, past the dozen or so cars. "I don't know what the hell it's supposed to mean." He shoots Everett a sidelong look, like they're in on a joke. But then also, it's a look that tells Everett he's irrelevant. "Well, whatever."

"Actually, I'd say the problem is more like the opposite," Everett says, after he thinks about it a minute, thinks about Joy pulling away from him little by little, day after day, year after year. "For a lot of people, anyway." Her fear of being with someone who truly loves her, that's the problem.

"What I do," Herb says, pointing toward the fishpond with his cigarette, "is think about myself like a fish. There are other fish around but I don't get in their way. And they don't get in mine. You never see fish tripping over each other, do you?"

21

"It's hard for me to imagine." Everett looks at the city beyond the trees, thinking of it as a big pond. "How do you do that? Keep them from tripping over you, I mean."

Herb shrugs.

Everett thinks about one of those other fish—Joy. He realizes that she's all he can think about, and he hasn't even considered what his life might be like without her, what it will be like if she doesn't change her mind. He relaxes and makes himself meditate on it. And right then, there is this image, a picture in his head of himself, alone, like it's been sitting there waiting. There was a time, when Joy was pregnant, when she had wanted him to make a go of woodworking, something he'd always done to relax because he was good at it almost without effort, but it had seemed too risky to him as a full-time job, what with a baby on the way. Remembering that, Everett sees that old dream of himself—outside, sawing and sanding, tan and fit and happy. It's like meeting up with a person he forgot he knew. But it also makes him think about how when they were married, he liked having Joy in the way, even when he was doing his own little projects. What they'd had together had mattered more than either of them had alone. He wants to explain this to Herb, crusty old Herb with his sour attitude and his solitary fishes, and he starts to think how.

"Herb?" They both turn and a small, dark-haired woman with a clipboard stands under the awning. She smiles, waits.

Herb grunts, takes one last deep drag. "Here we go again," he mutters. "I'll check you later." And he seems relieved, as if the only thing worse than the empty space is having Everett in it. Everett wonders if that's how Joy felt after the first night she kissed Larry.

"Yeah, okay," Everett says, and for a moment, he feels a cold panic in his chest as Herb brushes past, his heavy side-to-side movement already familiar somehow. After he's gone, Everett can still see the dark eyes, the pug nose, the small white scar below the bottom lip. How is it fair that his eyes can see so much? The images make him feel like he has a grasp of the person, which he never ever does.

He closes his eyes for a moment. Then he tries to focus on what the woman with the clipboard looks like. He tells himself, I am single now. There are other women, tons of them. He could be with her, with that woman. It's possible, in a scientific sense.

He leans against the wall for he doesn't know how long, wondering if there will ever be someone else and what she'll be like. Maybe it won't matter who he's with. Maybe all women are, in some way or another, the same as Joy. If only he wanted to find out. He stands there for a long time, listening to the trees, almost hearing their shadows pacing back and forth.

He goes to the pay phone just inside the door and he calls her at work. "It's an emergency," he says when he hears her voice. He has never used this tactic before; he knows that she will come.

He returns to the curb, sits down, and works on a duck call with his thumbs and a blade of grass, thinking how he'll teach it to Crystal.

Later, when the car drives up, crackling on the gravel, and swings into the most distant parking space, he watches her get out. She shuts the car door hard, and he sees that she's had her hair cut short; she wears a white t-shirt and jeans. He has to remember that she gave up the hygienist scrubs when she became an office manager. Is she worried about him? The thought sends a tingle along his arms.

He hasn't seen her up close in months. As she notices him on the curb, hesitates, and then walks closer, he studies her. Her features aren't exactly as he remembers them. It's like catching an unexpected look at his reflection in a store window and thinking That's what I look like?

"Hey," Everett says, giving her a nod, as if it's no big deal to see her.

"What's wrong with you?" she says, very business-like, and she steps onto the sidewalk, looking down at him where he sits. "Why are you here?"

He stands up, dusts off his hands. "What do you mean?" he says. He's in awe, all over again, by the physical presence of her—His body remembers what it felt like to hold her, the exact spots where he could feel her head, her breasts, her bones against him. He has to concentrate on his breath.

"What are you doing here?" she says, more emphatically now.

"I needed to get away."

"This isn't a bed and breakfast. And it isn't normal to call and say it's an emergency if you've decided to take a vacation." She has a hand on her hip and the other shading her eyes. He thinks now that her short hair makes her look smaller, like a fairy or something. She blinks up at him. "Have you been drinking? I swear, if Crystal's been at your apartment with you getting—"

"God, no. I would never." He thinks about Crystal's bedroom at his place, about the bedspread and the curtains he let her pick out at a department store, about the stuffed hippo on the bed. It's all so evocatively her—He has to shut the door during the week so the sight of it won't break his heart.

Joy squints, unconvinced.

He opens his hands as if to catch something fragile. "I just needed a little time away. I'm not a danger to anyone. I'm sure someone here can verify what I'm saying. If that's what you want." He gestures toward the building.

"I'm here to find out if my daughter's safe with you, and you haven't yet said a word that makes sense. So, yes, speaking with someone else would be fine."

"Fine." And then he says, "Is that the only reason you came? You weren't worried about me?"

"Oh, Everett, here we go," she says. "You know, I left a meeting at work to come here." She crosses her arms and shifts her feet.

Everett nods and looks down. "Nice toes," he says at last, pointing at her blue toenail polish. He notices her new sandals, too. Larry the professor knows all the small things about her now.

"Thanks," she says. And then: "You know, Everett, the way you act, the things you demand, it's like you're the only person who ever has feelings."

"Well, wasn't that the truth? In the end? When you were with what's-his-name, the asshole?" he says. But what angers him isn't really the affair. Instead, it's that she didn't try harder.

But then, also, maybe she's right that she did have feelings. He thinks back through the years of their marriage to watching her sleep, and calling her at work, and moping for her attention when she was watching TV or cuddling Crystal's cat, Snowy. He'd been desperate for her, even when things had been good, right back, actually, to that first day he stopped her when she was walking past his apartment. Maybe she's felt she was suffocating since the very beginning—maybe she's more like Stan than he is. And maybe he's always taken the wrong tack with her. His heart surges. "Come with me for a minute," he says and begins to walk to his car.

She makes her hands into fists. "What the fuck is this all about, Everett? I've got things—"

"Just come on."

They stop at the passenger door. "Put your hand out." He opens the door, reaches into the glove compartment, and finds the gun tucked between the folds of a road map. Holding it by the barrel, he offers it to her. "Point this at me. Ask me if I miss you."

"Jesus Christ, Everett. Why do you have that with you? What's happened to you?"

"Do it."

She pulls a Kleenex out of her back pocket, and he can see that her eyes have filled up. "I'm not a bad person, you know," she says and wipes at her nose and puts the tissue back in her pocket. She looks at the gun. "Would you please put that away?" she says.

Everett lets the pistol drop loosely to his side.

She looks at him with what seems like relief and deep sadness. She says, "I did end it all wrong. And I'm sorry. I've been wanting to tell you. Will you put away your gun?"

"Do you miss me?" he says.

She sighs. "Everett." She touches her hand to her forehead for a second and rubs back and forth, the way she always did when she was studying for her business-administration certificate. He imagines her palm is cool, like her hands always were, even in summer. He closes his eyes, imagining her touch. Isn't this, even just this one last troubled moment with her, what he's been wanting?

A dog barks somewhere down the hill and then crows squawk and flap through the branches on the other side of the parking lot. She squints into the spotty sunlight, her grayish eyes and faint laugh lines the same as always. But compared to the Joy in his mind, something is different. She weighs two pounds more or two pounds less? Something in the way she carries herself, the slope of her shoulders? He sets his gun down on the front seat and lets himself stare at her. "Joy," he says. "This thing with you and Larry won't last forever."

She sighs again, a little frustrated, but then she looks into the distance for a moment and laughs. "Actually," she says, "you're probably right." She takes a step back from the car and looks out over the new subdivision.

For a moment he isn't sure he's heard her right. His face goes slack. "What?" he says. Then he pauses, wanting to speak, but unable to. He forces himself to relax his shoulders and breath, tries to stand as he would stand if she weren't here, listens to the creaking of the trees.

She turns and looks at him for a long moment. Without thinking, he moves to her side, brings his hand up, and strokes the top of her honey-colored hair and then he watches the hand's movement like it isn't his, like even the sensation of her soft hair under his fingers is happening far away.

"Everett, you idiot," she says, looking at him, smiling sadly. "I do miss you. I miss many things about you. Of course I do."

He smiles back. "I'm glad." There's that feeling spreading across his chest again, that cold current. He thinks for a moment that it's the happiness he's been waiting for, the happiness that could only come from this, from her. But as it spreads into his arms, his throat, there is another feeling, a tingling realization in his stomach that it isn't happiness. In fact, it isn't anything he has felt before.

Joy smiles, raises her thumb and index finger in the shape of a gun. "So, punk, what about me? Tell me the truth. Do you miss me?"

It's a simple question, and he wants to give her the answers he has imagined for this moment of their reconciliation. But when he reaches for his feelings, all he can find is an empty, dry gnawing in his gut. Something that he has perhaps mistaken for longing, for love.

He smiles, wraps his fingers around her cool, pointed finger, and gently pushes it down. He shakes his head.

After Joy leaves, he stows the pistol again, gets his bag, and then he sits in the lobby. He tries to think of what he will say about himself. Of course, he can crib the language for that conversation; his book is with his clothes. Reaching down, he can feel the hardcover through the nylon of the bag. He listens hard for that desperate little voice in his head, the caterpillar fuzz vibration of it: How can I prove we belong together? He thinks about his mother's long pining for his father and he thinks, maybe what he's really been addicted to, maybe nearly all his life, is the hum of need.

Because now it is quiet. There is a terrible, unfamiliar, mysterious nothingness. Like staring into a cold black pond when the fish are hibernating in the deep, separated from one another and the bright world above, and all he can see is himself, shifting from one foot to the other, like if he moves fast enough, his reflection won't see him.

Black Lagoon

Dexter Gilliss and my brother, Charlie, were best friends all through grade school and high school, even though Dexter was my age—now seventeen—and Charlie was a year older. Dexter was there, that night last June, when Charlie dove off a retaining wall into Lake Iroquois. Charlie and Dexter had been drinking, celebrating Charlie's notice of an ROTC scholarship to Virginia Commonwealth College.

"You couldn't tell there wasn't much water," Dexter said later that night at the hospital, when we still thought Charlie might live. "If that stupid moon hadn't been full, reflecting all over the place, it wouldn't have looked so deep." He crossed his arms and refused the Baby Ruth candy bar his mother bought for him from the vending machine. She sat down on the long vinyl bench in the corner of the waiting room where Dexter's father and both of my parents already sat, huddled together. I remember thinking they looked like hamsters, like I was watching them through glass, like they weren't even people. I sat in a chair with green, stained upholstery, holding Charlie's keys in my hand—I'd lost mine and he'd loaned me his that afternoon at school. For the three hours my brother stayed alive, I watched Dexter pacing and explaining, his clothes stiff with lake water. I hated him.

Charlie died at 1:32 in the morning. We were given his favorite Fauquier County Track Club t-shirt, a pair of Levi's, a Swiss army knife, a wallet, and white Nike tennis shoes. When we all left the hospital and my parents and I drove away, I could see Dexter from my backseat window, still talking, cascades of words bubbling from his mouth, his hands punctuating the dark air. He was walking behind his parents toward their Buick station wagon, his mother and father holding hands tightly as if one of them might float away.

After they were out of sight, I turned and looked at the backs of my parents' heads, half moons over the headrests, shadows elongating and washing over me each time we passed under a streetlight.

Now, in December, Dexter and I, who have become boyfriend and girlfriend, make the forty-five minute drive to Washington, D.C., in his Skylark to watch *The Creature from the Black Lagoon* in 3-D. He makes us count potential police speed traps from the minute we leave Smoky Ordinary, Virginia, where we have both lived all our lives.

"How many is that?" Dexter says, pointing to a spot on the interstate median where the grass behind some bushes is well worn.

"Eight," I tell him, and write down the mile marker in his notebook. Dexter has gotten four speeding tickets and is worried he'll lose his license the next time, but also, there is a part of him that always wants to get away with something. If a guy in class or at the movies leaves his umbrella under his chair, Dexter will sneak up from behind and swipe it. Dexter might not even want the umbrella; he might just throw it in a box in the back of his closet that's full of umbrellas and other things he's stolen, like sunglasses and gloves—all things, it seems to me, that he can hide behind, that can keep him camouflaged if he's up to something or if he wants people to think he's up to something.

"I'd like to see those assholes catch me now," he says, and I look at the notebook pretending not to hear.

Sunday nights on this road always look the same: light traffic, the streetlights along I-66 visible for a mile or so ahead, looping and twisting like some nuclear snake. These five lanes are a curvy drainpipe that normally shoots a flood of cars into the District, but on Sundays is dry except for a few drops like us. When we pass Fair Oaks Mall, its pink sign in the black sky makes the night look colder than it really is. It has been unseasonably warm for December. That's what the man on the Weather Channel says to my mother, who keeps him on whenever she's home.

"I don't want any more surprises, not even with the weather," she told me one morning during the international traveler's advisory. She then sat patiently through a segment on flashfloods, waiting for the man at the desk to come back and show her the Mid-Atlantic states. "What you need to do is pretty simple, I think. You make sure you know what's coming and plan accordingly, Rachel," she said, though I could tell by the almost frightened way she looked at me that she knew as well as I did that there are some things you just can't plan for.

In the lane next to Dexter and me, two women wearing white uniforms, like the ones the orderlies at the hospital wore, pass us in a Chevrolet. They don't even have coats on over their uniforms, it's so warm. Theirs is the fourth car I've seen in which the people look at the road and do not talk; Dexter and I do not speak for five or ten minutes. He reaches over finally and mashes in the cigarette lighter, and when it pops back out, mashes it in again.

"God, I want to smoke," he says.

"Go ahead," I tell him, knowing that what he wants is permission. I know he keeps two cigarettes in the glove compartment. He used to smoke a pack and a half a day when Charlie was alive, and sometimes, when Charlie would say, "Hey Deathtrap, I'll race you to the end of your toes and back," Dexter would quit for several days. Charlie ran track and was health conscious, if you didn't count the French fries he ate after school or the people he hung out with, people like Dexter, who kept Ecstasy and aluminum baseball bats in the trunks of their cars. But Charlie was friends with both kinds of people at our school—the kind like Dexter as well as the kind on the track team, who wore Nike track jackets and $120 shoes and drove brand new cars to the meets instead of riding on the Spirit Bus.

On mornings after Dexter had supposedly given up cigarettes, he'd tell Charlie he forgot something and I'd see him run down alone to the Smoker's Room, an old shack in the woods behind our school. All during my junior year, I used to watch him from the window of the jewelry shop, my first period class. Because of urban sprawl, Smoky Ordinary has become a suburb of Washington, D.C.; Secret Service agents, government officials, and even the US Secretary of Agriculture live and pay taxes here, taxes that have bought our school its jewelry shop, its planetarium, and its photography darkroom equipment. Then there are the people who live and work in Smoky Ordinary, like my father, who owns the 84 Lumberyard. At the other end of the spectrum are people who work farther out in places like Halfway and Thoroughfare Gap—like Dexter's father, who's an auto mechanic out that way. His father is tall and wiry like a scarecrow, and Dexter would remind me of him when he'd race down that hill behind our school, his black trench coat trailing him like a cape. I made a pendant once that year of a flying blackbird that looked just like Dexter, and I showed it to Charlie.

"I knew you were sweet on Dexter," he said. "I've known it since you were in the third grade. I could tell whenever he'd spend the night. You'd wear that blue Cinderella nightgown and practice your ballet in the living room." Charlie knew long before I did. I didn't know until seventh grade, when I would watch from my bedroom window as the two of them threw the football. Dexter would motion me down to play and I would hide in the drapes until he forgot I was there. When we finally get to Key Theatre in northwest D.C., we find a parking space on the street a block down and then walk to the box office, the sound of our feet echoing off the closed shops, off Mattie's Wig Boutique and L&M Shoes. Dexter puts his arm around me and rubs the back of my hair, which I keep very short now. I put my arm around him, too, and we walk down the street like that, and Dexter begins to hum the Beatles' "Rita."

"I think you hum so you won't have to talk to me," I say.

"That's not true," he says, and squeezes me with the hand that's draped on my shoulder.

I get out my money because I always pay. Dexter hasn't been able to keep a job, partly because he wears his Ipod to work. He insists on wearing it, and then "zones out" (he says) to the music and, as a result, has gotten fired from Royale Drycleaners for wrecking a tuxedo, from Dairy Dream for breaking the swirly machine, and from Hampton Inn and El Ranchero Tacos for other things—all within the last four months. I, on the other hand, have been baby sitting our neighbors' children since October and plan to keep the job until we graduate from Smoky Ordinary High School in the spring. "You're so responsible," Dexter sometimes says to me, as if it's an accusation instead of a compliment.

Now, as I stand on Wisconsin Avenue, pulling a wad of one-dollar bills from my pocket and counting them, Dexter pokes my shoulder. "Rachel," he says, "Isn't that Lisa, Lisa and Cult Jam?" He points to the girl sitting in the box office and I squint down the block, but the wind whips up the warm smell of sewage and makes my eyes water. Lisa Pouncey is the only girl that Dexter and Charlie ever fought over. Charlie was dating her at the time of his death, but Lisa had refused to come to the funeral because she said it would be "too intense." As we get closer, I'm sure it's her because of the frosty pink lipstick and the gold hoop earring. Dexter and Charlie named her for an early '80s pop band they'd seen on VH-1. The lead singer's hair was nearly as huge and helmet-like as Lisa's. Who did that anymore?

"Yes, that's her," I tell him, and I look down at my money and find myself afraid to say, Maybe we should leave, Maybe we should do something else—things I would have said six months ago.

Mom says I've "lost my fire." When she comes home at four from her classroom at Thomas J. "Stonewall" Jackson Elementary School, she says, "I don't miss your smart mouth. I get enough of that from my fifth graders. But I sure wish you'd say something. Anything. Where's your spark?" At those times, I feel like saying to her, Where are your feelings? Because she never cries, though she has had a cold for months, as if the tears have been left no choice but to back up into her nose and chest. And she does insensitive things, like making mashed potatoes, Charlie's favorite dish, every Wednesday the way she used to, even though my father breaks down nearly every time she serves them. "I'm sorry, Richard," she says and puts the mashed potatoes back in the oven. I sometimes wonder what happens to all those potatoes.

I now find myself looking through the glass at Lisa Pouncey, who is staring at the green gem that is in the ring on her forefinger. I have the urge to say something nasty to her, like "Remember where that finger has been?" But I don't. "Two, please," I say, believing for a moment that if I don't say anything else, she might not recognize us.

"Lisa, Lisa and Cult Jam, is that you?" Dexter asks from behind me. She looks up slowly from the ticket button, which she has pushed twice while mouthing the words "one" and "two." When she sees Dexter, her eyes get big as if Bob Barker has told her to come on down. She begins to rise from her chair, but then seems to remember the glass and sits down again.

"Oh my God, you guys," she says, her voice very high. "How are you?" In that glowing glass booth, surrounded by darkness, she looks like she's in a lava lamp.

"It's been awfully quiet since you left Smoky Ordinary," Dexter says. Lisa graduated in Charlie's class and moved to Arlington because she said Smoky Ordinary was "fine if you like living in the sticks."

"How have you been?" Dexter says, and steps up to the booth like it's home plate. I see the tenderness in his face and a little bit of fury seeps up from somewhere inside me. I bang my fist on my leg as if that could stop it.

"You know, I've been pretty good," she says. She leans toward the window. "I've moved in with a couple of girls I met from working here. It's cool getting out of my parents' house." Lisa rolls her eyes. "You know how they can be," she says, looking at Dexter.

Back when Dexter and Charlie were fighting over Lisa, Dexter tried to sneak into her parents' house to have (he said) "a Certs Encounter" with her. And he did make it inside, but Lisa, who had invited him over, wasn't home, and her parents mistook him for a prowler and called the police. Dexter ran to our house and I had to be the one to tell him that Lisa was with Charlie—they'd gone to a party one of his friends from the track team was throwing at the country club.

"If he wasn't my friend . . .," Dexter had said, panting from his run. I stepped outside and he put his hand on my shoulder and leaned on me. "Just let me catch my breath," he told me, sweat thick on his face and neck.

"I don't think he knew about your plans," I said. We sat down on the front steps together and waited for Charlie to come home. When Charlie came up the walk, he was whistling; he stopped when he saw Dexter and the expression on his face.

"What?" Charlie said, confused, his happy face shining at us in the glow of the porch light.

"Nothing," Dexter said. "Forget it." He pulled a cigarette out of his shirt pocket, put it to his mouth, and went to light it. He stared at the flame, as if it were talking to him. "Shit," he said, tossing the unlit cigarette on the ground. The flame disappeared back inside the lighter, taking the orange cast off Dexter's face. I caught myself biting my fingernails, something I was trying to quit doing, and I tried to find a way to hide the jagged cuticles and nubby tips, though I knew Dexter wouldn't notice, wouldn't look at them, wouldn't do anything except think about Lisa on his long walk home.

"We're going to miss the beginning," I say now to Dexter, who's watching Lisa through the glass of the ticket window.

"Right," he says, sounding drunk, as if he's heard me without really listening. Lisa sits upright suddenly in the chair and looks afraid that we might walk away.

"My roommates and I are having a party on Friday and I'd love for you . . . both of you . . . to come," she says, and looks at me for the first time. "I even have an invitation in here somewhere." She disappears for a moment as she bends down and rifles through some papers. Somebody behind us starts to grumble about the show starting. "Here it is." She sits up again, her hair even bigger than it was before and two of the buttons on her blouse having popped open so that we can see half her breasts. She pushes a small white paper through the hole and Dexter reaches past me to take it.

"Cool," he says. "We'll try to make it." I look at him and try to figure out whether he remembers that I have to work on Friday. If he remembers, I can't tell.

"Hey, you guys," Lisa says. "Don't worry about the tickets. Just go on in." The wind picks up just then and I wonder if it's a message about accepting gifts from people you don't like, but we go in anyway, sitting way over on the right side in the back so the people in the projection booth can't see us. Dexter likes to bring his own drinks, Cokes or sometimes Jim Beam, and also he just doesn't like to be watched.

As we wait for the movie to start, we eat our greasy popcorn. There are only five other people in the theater. "Are you going to that party by yourself?" I say quietly as the lights begin to dim and the music starts for the cartoon of the dancing soda cups and candy boxes. Dexter doesn't hear me.

"Hey, it's starting," he says, and settles into his chair and puts on his 3-D glasses. He pulls a flask of Jim Beam from the back of his pants, takes a swallow, and then offers it to me.

I shake my head no.

"This is going to be good," he says.

The credits roll on a background of gray smoke, and a booming voice says, "In the beginning, God created the heaven and the earth, the earth without form and void." Then, there is an explosion and chunks of earth fly out from the screen.

"Cool," Dexter mutters, but it doesn't seem like he's talking to me. Through the glasses, I can see the movie screen and the glint of light from Dexter's glasses. I can see Dexter settling into his chair. I sit with my hand on my knee, hoping Dexter might take it.

In the movie, the scientists, on the trail of some prehistoric bones, are bickering about whether to venture into the black lagoon.

"There's only one thing," Scientist David says. "Going into unexplored territory with a woman."

"I'm not afraid, David, and we've come this far," the woman says. She's packed into a pair of white shorts and wiping away the sweat on her cleavage.

Normally, Dexter whispers to me about women like her, saying something like, "Wearing an outfit like that isn't very scientific. Think how many places the swamp water can get in." Sometimes, he offers to get more popcorn, too, but tonight he does not move.

He watches the boat arrive at the black lagoon, the scientist go below deck to confer, and the woman strips down to a white bathing suit and goes for a swim. He watches her the way he used to watch me just before Charlie died. Once Lisa had dumped Dexter for Charlie, Dexter began to notice me; he would bring his green sleeping bag over and sleep on Charlie's floor, and when I would walk past Charlie's room in the morning after my shower, he would open his eyes just a little, just enough to see me.

The creature in the movie had been appearing next to the boat, but nobody knows it, and he follows the woman on her swim. For five minutes or more, we watch underwater scenes of the woman swimming while the creature swims parallel right beneath her, like some distorted mirror image. "Great costume, huh?" I say finally, gesturing to the strangely human creature on the screen, who looks like a cross between a fish and a giant infant. Dexter doesn't look at me. "How do you like that costume?" I say again, irritated.

"Great," he says, but like he doesn't care, and I don't speak to him again for the rest of the movie. At the end, when the creature, full of knife and spear gun wounds, swims to the bottom of the lagoon to hide in the seaweed, I turn away because he's gone limp and I don't want to see him like that, floating the way Charlie must have, his body stunned and full of deep wounds. When I look back at the screen, the camera is looking at the creature from below, and he looks like a dead astronaut floating toward a sun millions of miles away. The screen goes black and Dexter and I both leave our glasses on until the lights come up. Through one red lens and one blue lens, I look at Dexter, a pinkish shadow beside me, tapping his foot on the candy-stained floor.

Outside, it has gotten foggy. Charlie would have said, if it were at a time when he was mad at Dexter, that the fog was as thick as Dexter's head. The air lurks, heavy and wet, and the box office has a halo of light that seems to lure Dexter toward it. I follow slowly.

"So, how do I get to your house?" Dexter says to Lisa when he gets to the window. She gives him directions, but he doesn't understand, so he puts his hand through the hole and she writes her phone number on it. She has manicured pink fingernails, I notice, as her slender fingers grip the pen and she concentrates on writing the number. I try to imagine her hand holding Charlie's, and I find myself remembering an evening last May when I was rocking on our porch swing, thinking of Dexter, as I often did, and Charlie came out and sat down next to me.

"I like her, and she's sexy, but I don't know how to talk to her," he said. He was looking out over the yard, his muscular legs pushing the swing faster than I pushed it by myself.

"Well," I said after a minute, "maybe talk is not as important as it seems."

"Maybe," Charlie told me, "but it's getting lonely to be with her." He looked up at the moon, which was nearly full and shining silver like still water. He put his arm on the back of the swing behind me and let me push for a while. We heard police sirens then, a few blocks over.

"Dexter," we both said at the same time, and Charlie laughed. It was what we both thought because it was the sound of trouble.

Dexter is looking at the phone number written in red on his palm, and Lisa twirls her pen between her fingers like a gunslinger. They say their good-byes and then Dexter turns toward me as if for the first time tonight he is seeing me as more than a ghost.

"Ready?" he says. I don't say anything, but start walking with him toward the car. It's late and the traffic has thinned even more. I can see Dexter's car under a streetlight two blocks away. "Who do you think will be at that party?" he asks me.

Well, Lisa, for one, I want to say, but shrug my shoulders instead. Dexter doesn't notice. He lags behind me a little in the shadows as if he might evaporate in the moist air, and maybe it's fear that he'll disappear that allows me to speak. "What is it you're afraid to say?" I ask him.

"Nothing," he says, looking at me as if waking from a dream, as if he could still be that boy who spent the night at our house in a bright green sleeping bag. He squints like I'm hard to see. "What are you talking about?"

I'm afraid to say nothing, too, I think to myself as Dexter opens the car door for me and then slams it shut once I am inside. The air sealed in the car with me is humid with the smell of vinyl and Dexter's old cigarettes, and I watch Dexter walk around to his side. The streetlight shines down on him, and I can see the moisture flying around in the air over his head, disturbed by the flap of his clothing and the long strides of his arms and legs. As he gets in the car and shuts the door, I watch him fumble with his keys, one hand on the steering wheel, his eyes directed forward.

I follow his gaze down the block to the neon L&M Shoes sign that glows red through the mist, but when I look back at him, he seems to be staring straight into the windshield, not seeing anything. And the reality is, he is always leaving one space and arriving in another, like the dark clouds on TV weather maps that swirl past in satellite pictures. And I'm in one of those spaces he's already left. I'm closed up inside for protection, like that creature swimming for all those years in that lagoon. I think I'd become that sort of person even before Charlie died, but I couldn't see it then. Now, I'm lit up to myself the way the scientist lit up the creature at the end of the movie, when he was hiding from them in the seaweed.

"Ready?" he says, and when I nod, he starts the car. I lean toward the passenger window and look into the fog, imagining I can see the moisture particles nestled against the car, imagining how they'll tumble inward when we drive away.

Permanent Resident

Even with the grainy picture on the screen of the old motel TV, Alicia could see that the man playing Jesus in the Saturday morning movie, supposedly walking on water, actually stood on a square of plexi-glass. It was like her physics teacher, Ms. Hastings, was always saying—most magic was a matter of using a suitable formula or the right apparatus.

On the other side of the room—all of six feet away—Alicia's mother, Louise, sighed and picked up the phone to get a line outside the Valley View Motor Lodge. "It's an emergency," her mother said to the desk clerk. Her voice lacked any urgency. "This is Louise Mayberry," she said. "My boyfriend is in trouble, and I need you to put me through to the police." She rolled her eyes at Alicia. "Yes, of course I know I could dial 911. Now, could you put me through?" It occurred to Alicia, as she met her mother's look of boredom with a stare, that for Louise's problems, magic wouldn't help. What her mother needed was something more like a tsunami—something that would wipe the slate clean. Well, maybe she was about to get it.

Louise wrinkled her brow as she finally got the police on the line. She told the story, listened, and then she hung up. "Turns out this is a bad time to go nuts," she told Alicia. The Fauquier County police, tied up with the Halloween Parade and the murder of a city councilman, were indeed concerned that her boyfriend wanted to kill himself. They'd go over to the house as soon as possible. Just not yet. "I think this is some sort of sign," Louise said, leaning her blonde head on her knees. "Do you want to go now?"

Louise's boyfriend, Palmer, whose house she and Alicia had lived in until one thirty that morning, had holed up in the bathroom the night before with his Army-issued .45. Louise hadn't expressed much in the way of sympathy. She refused, she said, to keep her daughter in such a situation, and had ordered Alicia to pack a bag. Alicia had felt oddly naked with her welfare brought into it; she was an observer of her mother's life, as she liked to think of it, a researcher more than a daughter anymore, and it felt all wrong to be involved with her subject.

"It's not a sign. It's clear evidence," Alicia said. "Well, thank you for calling them. It just tells us there's not going to be any magical solution. We'll be the ones to fix this. Or not." She reached for her backpack, unzipped it, and peered in at the stack of folded clothes, two meticulously matched outfits, complete with earrings, scotch-taped to the inside of the blouses. One pair was dressy, silver with purple stones, perfect for her college interview, set to begin in ninety minutes. Earlier, in the darkness of her room, she had moved in a methodical way from her dresser to her closet, removing articles, but she could not remember having any specific thoughts about what she was doing. "Honestly, I don't know how I can go through an interview without knowing what's happened to Palmer," she said, partly to herself.

"We're not going back to that house without the police," Louise said. "It's too serious." She yawned. "And for now, they're busy. So that's the end of the story." Even though it was warm for October, Louise tugged the blankets over her black jeans. She glanced at the chipped yellow paint on the wall and then out the glass door at the half-filled pool, but she seemed not to see any of it. "You aren't making an excuse, are you? You still want to go to that school, don't you?"

"Of course I do," Alicia snapped. "But there are some responsibilities to think about."

Louise gazed from behind her shaggy hair, delicate wrinkles reaching for her temples. "Relax," she said.

Alicia plucked the interview clothes from the backpack and turned away. She imagined Monday morning saying to Heather Berkman, her friend from history: "She finally did it. She was an ass and acted like she didn't care, and sure enough, he did himself in."

As soon as Alicia had this thought, she felt bad for thinking the worst, and for letting anger toward her mother get mixed up with thoughts about Palmer, who, she knew, might be truly ill, in a way she shouldn't joke about. Alicia liked Palmer; he was by far the best boyfriend Louise had found anywhere in the Southeast. She remembered Buck Gumm, a salesman in Birmingham who had made them both wash their hands all the time; Sonny Watkins, a Marine sergeant in Fayetteville who had accused Louise of malicious poisoning when she set off a flea bomb and forgot to cover the butter; Murphy Lister, a roofer in Charleston, who had watched TV in bikini briefs after work and then acted hurt that fourteen year-old Alicia wouldn't introduce him to her friends. There were several others. Louise had broken up with all of them within a year and then moved someplace else, claiming she'd heard about better jobs or cheaper rents in Macon or Lexington or Jackson. She had been dating Palmer for eight months, they had been living with him for seven, but until his meltdown last night, nothing had gone quite as badly as it normally did. Palmer never grabbed Louise's rump as if she were a waitress at Hooters. He didn't screech out of the driveway at two a.m., when, after six months, Louise had shouted that she wouldn't sleep with him anymore and moved into Alicia's room. He didn't bring home other, younger girls or talk to them on the phone. Instead, when he got to feeling morose, he combed through boxes in the attic, sorting and resorting the belongings of Jay Troxler, his friend from the Special Forces who got killed when they were stationed together—officially in Honduras, actually in El Salvador. He studied photos and newspaper clippings until they wilted in his warm hand.

"I'm as relaxed as I need to be," Alicia said to her mother, and then gathered the lists of sample interview questions she'd gotten from her guidance counselor, Mr. Meagle. She would have to take the next half hour to study them under the dim, nicotine-stained lamp beside the bed she had shared with Louise. Though she had studied under bad circumstances before, she wondered if any of them topped this. There was the time she had studied for her Latin final during the dance party to celebrate Murphy's drunk-driving acquittal. And there was the time that Alicia had finished the last week of school in a tent with her mother because the boyfriend of the day had become "stressed out"—he'd thrown a kitchen chair through the passenger window of her car. There was a while, when Alicia was trying to cut herself some slack, when she called it an accomplishment enough simply to turn in her homework without tacking on a story. The kinds of things other kids used as excuses were embarrassingly weak.

Alicia scrutinized the room around her—the brown drapes, the dusty heating unit protruding from the wall, the TV stand chained to an eye hook on the dresser beside it. "Just once, when you leave a boyfriend, I'd like to stay at the Ramada Inn," she said.

Louise looked up from the Northern Virginia Apartment Guide she'd found in a drawer of the night stand. Her look of incomprehension turned into a nervous laugh. "I haven't left Palmer," she said, waving the book. "This is—," She fanned the pages with her thumb. "I was just glancing through this."

"And I was trying to be funny," Alicia said. "You know? Ha ha?" She sat at the foot of the bed and began to pull on a pair of nude pantyhose.

She really hadn't meant it as a joke. What she had really intended to do was make Louise feel bad, which she was growing better at doing, though in this case she wasn't sure if it had worked or if she'd wanted it to after all. Louise hadn't been herself lately. She'd been studying the help-wanted classifieds in *The Washington Post* and she hadn't talked even once about moving to a different city. She never hummed Beach Boys songs in the shower anymore and she'd stopped making eggs for Alicia and Palmer, the way she usually made eggs every evening for her other boyfriends and Alicia, feigning great affection until she and Alicia moved out. Instead, she sat on the front stoop in the afternoons, barefoot, toeing the mulch around the azaleas, as if she might silently dive in and swim across adjoining lawns until she was gone, gone out of sight. Yet she didn't go. One day last week, Alicia had been so distracted by Louise's peculiar stillness, wondering whether they would be living with Palmer when she got home from school, that she forgot to bring her gym shorts in her school bag and got a zero for the day in P.E. She had not gotten a zero on anything in five years.

After another minute of watching Alicia dress, Louise said, "Okay, I've got one: How do they know that Jesus was bad at math?"

"How?" Alicia said.

"He got nailed to the plus sign."

Alicia stood to zip her skirt. "Geez. That's bad." She smiled in spite of herself.

Louise liked religious jokes, particularly Catholic ones, maybe because her own mother had managed to get pregnant with Louise just before she was to go off to a convent. Because Louise's mother didn't take up with the father, a local handyman, and because her family disowned her, Louise had grown up with no adults around her at all except her mother, a woman who saw visions of the Virgin Mary and St. Theresa of Avila in the steam from boiling water. Later, when Louise was a teenager, the handyman took to rubbing against her whenever he saw her alone in the aisle of a store or at a park. "I always wondered if he knew who I was," Louise had told Alicia once, "or if he did that to all kinds of people." Alicia wanted to know which Louise thought was better—if he knew or if he didn't. It seemed like there should be a third, less obvious but simple answer, like in the Japanese koans Alicia learned about in social studies.

Alicia bent down to put on her tan shoes, and she felt a little queasy. She hadn't eaten anything since last night's frozen turkey pot pie. It occurred to her that Louise hadn't eaten anything either; low blood sugar sometimes caused Louise to get migraines. If that happened, they could end up in the hotel room with the lights off for a couple of days. "Do you want something from the vending machine before we go?" Alicia asked.

"No, thanks," said Louise. She had put aside the apartment listings and was tracing her finger down a page in the phone book, looking for people who shared her last name, something she always did in motels. In the past, it had seemed to Alicia that she did it because she wanted to feel like there was at least one avenue left to take, like somewhere there were people who would take her in if things got really bad. Now, that fantasy didn't seem very useful, though, because things were really bad, in a new way, and strangers were not going to be any help. Maybe, Alicia thought, it was that Louise liked to imagine those other Mayberrys leading productive lives, having published phone numbers and stable addresses all their own. Maybe Louise imagined her own name in there. "You could hand me my cigarettes," she said, reaching out absently, and Alicia gave her the Winstons from the dresser.

Alicia's own last name was Brock, but she knew little about her father, just that he was the one man Louise had married, and that he had died in a motorcycle accident when Alicia was three. Sometimes, especially when she'd had a little to drink, Louise would speculate about what Alicia's father would be doing now if he were alive. "He would have loved the internet," she'd said once, with Palmer in the room. "And so maybe he'd finally have a decent job, and we'd all go out for steak dinners on the weekends."

Alicia wanted to ask Louise to speculate about what Palmer himself might be doing right then, but her mother had escaped so deeply into the pages on her lap that even her own fingers lighting the cigarette in her puckered lips didn't lure her eyes away. It was rare for Louise to experience complete absorption, to not be on the move, and so Alicia sank into the shabby red chair in the corner and watched her, saddened by what her mother would wake to when she looked up.

Alicia closed her eyes and thought about the shock she'd had the night before, when, getting up to use the bathroom, she had walked in on Palmer by mistake. He sat on the toilet lid wearing his favorite clothes, as if he were ready to go outside and rake leaves—painter's pants, a green windbreaker, and a Washington Redskins ball cap—and he had his .45 in his lap.

Alicia understood his intentions right away because she knew about the anniversary of his friend Jay Troxler's death, and she knew that the crescent-shaped scar on Palmer's neck was from the self-inflicted wound that had gotten him discharged from the Army. And Alicia had noted that Palmer had been drinking more lately, and calling his mother, and cleaning his guns nearly every day—things he hadn't done at all when he'd first met Louise and Alicia. Yet, in spite of all the days of Palmer giving these signs, the possibility that he would actually take this kind of action had seemed remote to Alicia, like the fact that she would get old someday or, even less plausible, that Louise would.

Palmer had looked surprised and guilty when Alicia walked into the bathroom, almost as if he had been the one to walk in on her. "I wouldn't have done anything while you were here," he'd mumbled. He was drunk.

"Well," she said, reaching for words she couldn't find. Settling for others. "Some comfort. I'm not going anywhere tonight."

"But it's Friday," he said. "Where are your friends?"

"I'm getting ready for my interview."

"UVA?" he drawled, absently touching the gun.

"Yeah," she said. And then: "Palmer, come on. What are you doing?"

"You'll do great," he said. "They'd be crazy not to take you. Now, you look at a sad sack like me, on the other hand—"

"Palmer..." Alicia had begun, not knowing what she would say that might take him off this frightening track. He was a tall, muscular man, and there was no chance she could overpower him. But he was also shy, with slender, tapered wrists and ankles, and he always paused before he spoke, like he was on the verge of saying something that had been on his mind a long time. Louise had met him in the parking lot of the Safeway, where he'd helped her round up some runaway oranges that had rolled from a ripped paper sack, then started to walk off to his own car. And so, from the start, Alicia had trusted him more than the men who approached Louise in diners or bars with some tired line, or worse yet, their real intentions. "Mom doesn't mean to be hurting you," Alicia finally said. "Don't let her get to you like this. And anyway, she's not worth it," she added.

Palmer ran a hand through his thick, sandy hair. "You know that's not true," he told her. "I know you don't believe that." Palmer's words had made her turn away for a moment, embarrassed because, when it came down to it, she didn't know how she felt about her mother.

"It's just that, you know how she is," Alicia said then, and rubbed her fingertips on her forehead because she thought she might do something—plead or cry or otherwise act foolish. "Can't you just give it a little more time? I'll talk to her. I'll try to help." She slid down the hallway wall until she was on the floor, the tile warm and gritty.

"I've thought about things from every direction," Palmer said, and wiped his face with the collar of his jacket. "You know this isn't about you, right? And maybe it's not even about your mother. There's just something wrong," he said, pointing to himself.

Alicia pictured the way he held his racket whenever she convinced him to play paddle ball with her in the driveway, his arm stiff and stuck out to the side like a broken wing. They were his paddles, ones she had found in the closet, and Alicia had never been very athletic, but it was all right with him. He never preached at her about sports or tried to teach her things. And yet she felt he welcomed her in front of a Redskins game just by the way he caught her up on the action, and then nestled deeper into the game. She thought about the way he looked at the dusky sky sometimes out on the driveway, mouth in a slight, sad grin, cheeks slack, eyes squinted like they were trying to hold something. She would watch him from inside the house and wonder what he saw in the tight band of pink-orange clouds. Something lost. And then, suddenly, Alicia's mother would be home from her job as a telemarketer at Houseman Vinyl Siding, and she would be standing in the hallway in front of Alicia, yelling at her for not starting dinner, and yelling at Palmer to come in and help.

Louise's exits, at least on her side, were normally silent. With this departure, last night, she'd been a storm of words. She'd seen the bathroom light, had come to see what was happening, and in a moment had made her decision. She pulled Alicia up from the floor and pushed her back down the hall. Alicia started to cry, and Louise stomped her foot. "And damn you for making me worry like this," she shouted at Palmer. It pisses me off." Most of what else she'd said Alicia couldn't remember.

"What time is it?" her mother was asking now, the phone book cast aside, a sprawled heap, like a baby blanket Alicia had seen once along the interstate. Without waiting for an answer, Louise said, "All right. Let's get going."

When Louise came back to the room from checking out, Alicia looked at her watch—twenty-five minutes before her interview. "What's the guy's name again?" Louise said, swinging her fringed black bag as they walked to the car. The morning light cast a weak glow on Louise's honey-colored hair and pink shirt, and Alicia could see that the switch of her hips lacked the usual eagerness. And wasn't this, in part, what Alicia had always wanted? For her mother to walk (and also talk, cook, shop, and dress) like a normal thirty-five-year-old person? So why was it making her feel so weird?

"I told you three times already," Alicia said. "It's Jim Nealy. He's going to be in the lobby. You'll get to meet him, and then you can wait for me there."

Alicia had scored a 1460 when she took her SAT's, and several good schools out of state had given her special attention, but Alicia really wanted to go to UVA, partly so that she could come home on breaks to Palmer's little stucco house. It was hard to imagine Louise all settled in someplace, the boxes in the closet unpacked, her makeup and brushes on the bathroom counter instead of in her small travel case, her high heels and detective novels scattered through the house. But maybe, she'd thought, because Palmer wanted that, too, it could happen.

Unlike Louise's other boyfriends, Palmer had carefully cleared out space in the cupboards and he was always removing Louise's dishes and silverware from a box in the pantry; each time, she washed them, wrapped them in newspaper, and returned them. It was like a little dance they had choreographed together, the way it kept happening the same way. And Louise would never talk to him about anything beyond a month in the future, falling silent when he discussed plans for her birthday in May or Alicia's graduation in June. Sometimes, Alicia imagined she could come back to Palmer's house even if Louise wasn't there and she imagined how much more peaceful the house would be. But this thought always made her feel guilty. And also a little sad—maybe Palmer wouldn't want her around if not for Louise.

Alicia threw her backpack onto the floor of the car and got in, the papers she hadn't studied still in her hand. Louise drove down Jefferson for several miles, seeming to hit every red light, past a man selling chain-saw sculptures and cider, past a group of three women in matching "Check out my ghoulish figure" sweatshirts, and then she swerved into the Starvin' Marvin parking lot. "There's no time for coffee," Alicia said, pointing to her watch.

"I want to call the police again," Louise said.

"Now you decide to be worried about Palmer?" Alicia said. "Could you have any worse sense of timing?"

Her mother shrugged. She parked and used the payphone directly in front of the car, hunching forward for privacy from the customers hurrying in and out of the building. She looked to Alicia like a cat she had seen outside of a Shoney's once who curved her spine around her kittens like that would be enough to keep out the traffic noise and the curious children. When she got back in, she told Alicia that the police had finally relented. "You can quit worrying about him. They said they'd be able to go over there in about an hour."

"Oh good. That'll be right on time if he hurt himself six hours ago," Alicia said. She tried, unsuccessfully, to picture Palmer sitting right now at the breakfast table, as if it were a normal morning. Even though he'd been on disability for several years for the Army injury, he always set his alarm so he could eat breakfast with Alicia before school. She told him he didn't have to, that he could sleep late like Louise, who worked into the evening, but he always appeared as she ate her cereal, in his ratty gray bathrobe and with his hair standing in asymmetrical horns. Sometimes, lately, he would have a shot of Scotch and always he read to her from the newspaper. Once, he'd read to her a story about a woman who greased the floors in an attempt to kill her one-legged boyfriend. "Well, at least that's creative," Palmer had said. "People usually kill each other in very predictable ways." Alicia wondered now if he'd been right about the ways people hurt each other and themselves. It seemed like even with all the evidence in the world, maybe it was only predictable after the fact.

By the time Louise pulled into the Embassy Suites parking lot, they were five minutes late, and Alicia's palms had dampened the lists of sample questions. As they walked toward the gold and plate-glass hotel front, Louise put her arm around Alicia. "Don't worry," she said. "You always worry too much."

But when Alicia looked, she saw that Louise's face was tight and colorless. She nodded solemnly and pulled ahead of her mother into the revolving door. Inside, she spotted Jim Nealy right away; he was the only businessman sitting in a long row of plush orange chairs by the wall. He was probably in his forties, and he had reddish hair and a neatly trimmed beard. He appeared to recognize her as well, and he got up and walked toward them.

"Hello," he said, extending his hand. He wore chinos and a UVA golf shirt, casual attire, like he'd advised her was appropriate for the interview, but he still looked dressed up. That was money, Alicia thought. After he told them he liked to be called Jim, he said, "Well, let's go talk, shall we?" and suggested they go to the hotel cafe. He shook Louise's hand, and they walked away from her. As they strolled through the lobby, past the floor-to-ceiling windows, Jim said, "You two look like you could be sisters."

So many different men had said this to them before. Alicia smiled with one side of her mouth, as if she couldn't muster the strength to smile with both. "Well, my mom's growing up so fast," she half-heartedly joked.

"And into such a fine young lady," Jim said, grinning at Alicia. Alicia knew she should be smiling back, but there was a familiar vacant way he looked at her that said it really wouldn't matter if she did or not.

After they settled at a table, Jim ordered coffee for himself and tea for Alicia, and she examined the atrium around them, trees growing toward the skylights six floors up, the sound of water diffusing the voices of clip-winged parrots in the branches nearby. Even though she had always dreamed of staying in a hotel like this, now she found the extravagance made her feel ashamed. Could she, or anyone else, deserve all this—especially with Palmer like he was? She wanted to go back to the lobby and tell her mother to go after him now, to come back for her later.

Jim pulled a file from his briefcase; it was full of papers pertaining to Alicia's application. "I feel like I know a lot about you already." He touched the file with his pink, uncalloused hands. Alicia thought she detected a thin band of pale skin on his ring finger. "I just want to give you the opportunity to fill in more details."

"Okay," Alicia said and looked at the next table, where a young woman in a black business suit was sitting, someone only three or four years older than Alicia. The woman was blowing on her coffee and gazing past them, past an ice sculpture of a pelican, past an abandoned cart full of luggage, through the glass doors lit up with full morning sun, maybe all the way through the parking lot and past Palmer's house, toward something else. But what? The woman looked like someone with no limits on her future. Meanwhile, Alicia felt like when she took sex education in fifth grade—like she had deciphered a secret code and maybe life would have been easier if she hadn't.

"It says here," Jim continued, "that you've participated in a number of extra-curricular activities. And it's a terrific list, especially for someone so new to the school. Are there any that you didn't include on this list? Maybe there are some less official ones that you think should have some bearing on your application."

Alicia mulled this over for a moment, but what came to mind instead was when she buried Palmer's Jim Beam in the backyard the weekend before, and the way he'd methodically searched the house and yard until he found the freshly filled hole. He had seemed almost disappointed as he brushed off the bottle and took a long pull. Then, she thought about sitting in the parking lot with her friends after school, listening to music and to stories about things they did before she moved to Smoky Ordinary, Virginia, in March. She had memorized those stories like schoolwork so that she could imagine them as her own.

Mr. Meagle had reminded her to breathe deeply, answer hard questions with her instincts, and say she didn't know when that was the truth. She tried, but just step number one, breathing deeply, made her think about Martin Nix, a boy she left behind in Nashville, and the way he had kissed her after that last French Club meeting, the way she had gasped for breath and vowed to come back for him. During the seven-hour ride in the U-haul, unable to think about anything else but unable to tell Louise the truth, she had tried to teach her all the French she knew. But they ended up singing "American Pie" and "Blue Bayou" instead, because Louise said it bored her to just count to a hundred and practice saying hello and goodbye. Alicia thought about how those long moves between cities were secretly her favorite times, because Louise was always happy—humming, chattering about the scenery, and digging for change in the bottom of her purse so they could stop for soft-serve ice cream cones.

She wondered where that Louise was and if she'd ever be back. Alicia's mouth hung open. She moved her lips, willing words to travel from her brain. What Alicia finally said to Jim was, "I was on the decorations committee for Homecoming this year." She glanced nervously at the woman at the next table, wishing she were Louise, who had taught her how to make paper swans for the tables, and who had chaperoned the dance with Palmer, the two of them slow dancing to "Desperado" near where the lunch line normally was. Alicia had gone to the dance with her science partner, Pat Huff, but had mostly thought about how she couldn't remember exactly what Martin Nix looked like anymore. "There was a mythology theme, and a bunch of us in the Classics Club really got into it. We made a giant Hercules, so I guess it's a good thing our team won. It would have seemed silly." She smiled in a way that she hoped seemed relaxed and confident.

Jim gave no sign that she'd answered well. "Tell me a little more about why you want to attend UVA," he asked, and then rested his temple on two fingers, as if he was preparing to listen very closely. Alicia thought about her desire to make Palmer's house her home, to have something to put down under "permanent residence" if she was asked. Could this be the kind of candor that Mr. Meagle was suggesting? But then for the first time, she allowed herself to imagine that Palmer was already dead, that he had never made it out of that bathroom. She wondered whether they would have to identify his body and she pictured his naked feet sticking out from under a sheet, the same way they stuck out from under his bathrobe when he lay on the kitchen floor some mornings to tinker with the rusty pipes. She could see him at his funeral, pasty and pale, thick rugged hands stacked and folded like delicate handkerchiefs, his mother and sisters crying, Louise smoking out in the hall and maybe cleaning out her purse. Then Alicia was afraid that God or whoever might mistake her thoughts for a wish and she felt sick again, a bitterness in her throat. With Palmer dead, she herself would be a ghost, floating in and out of classes at some university. It didn't matter which one.

"From what I can tell, UVA is a place where people live together and also work together—they feel like they're part of something important," Alicia said. She shivered, though she wasn't exactly cold. She took a long drink of water in an effort to collect herself and maybe to wash back the truth—that she didn't actually want the life she'd been living to change. Beyond being the one constantly beloved thing in Louise's life, what was she? Could she even become part of something else? "I want that," she told Jim. "But then, also, I want to be independent—" The woman at the next table, looking up suddenly from her coffee, knocked the sugar tray onto the floor with her elbow. Jim helped her pick up the packets. When he sat up and smiled again, Alicia said, "And it seems like—it seems like you can have it both ways at UVA."

At this Jim lit up, looked proud, and said, "That's exactly right."

Alicia exhaled for the first time in what seemed like hours. It became a little easier then to answer his questions, to focus on what he was asking her, and when the interview was over, Jim shook Alicia's hand as if she'd done okay. They walked back out to the lobby, where Alicia's mother stood up from one of the couches.

"Maybe I'll see you at that Parents' Weekend thing," Louise said and smiled weakly.

"I hope so," he said, with what seemed to Alicia like a hint of flirtation.

But Louise didn't respond by blushing or averting her eyes bashfully or making a bold remark of her own, things Alicia had seen her do many times. Instead, she shook his hand and looked at him without interest, focusing more on her purse, which had slid off her shoulder. As they watched his broad form disappear into the elevator, Louise touched Alicia's arm and started to ask how it had gone, but Alicia interrupted her. "It's not important, Mom. Let's see about Palmer."

Louise looked a little hurt, but then she perked up. "Okay. Let's go," she said.

They walked back to the car, and neither of them spoke on the drive through the Virginia suburbs, past the DMV where Louise had registered the car, past the Hardees where some of Alicia's friends worked, past semi-familiar banks and churches and cafes, past acres and acres of new housing developments, back to the old two-bedroom house they shared with Palmer.

When they turned onto South Ross Street, where they lived, Alicia saw the two squad cars right away, their lights flashing. "Oh, God," she said. A small group of neighbors was gathered across the street partway down the block—the nurse from two doors down, and her mother-in-law with the silvery wig, the guy with the big belly who always fixed things he found in other people's trash, the two skinny kids from next door, and the guy from the Dairy Queen in his uniform. They chattered excitedly, seeming to act out wild scenarios with their hands. And then they saw Louise's car approaching and fell silent.

"Oh, God," Louise echoed, and Alicia turned from the neighbors and followed Louise's eyes to where, half-obscured by a tall hedge, an ambulance was parked in the neighbor's yard.

She pulled up behind one of the police cars, and an irritated officer tried to wave her away. "I live there," she said out the window and jumped out of the car and began to move toward the house, Alicia following. The policeman caught Louise's wrist and began to say something, but Alicia couldn't comprehend his words amid the noise of what she saw—the bright yellow ambulance , two men in orange jumpsuits waiting with a gurney with a medical box and oxygen tank on top of it, the geraniums Palmer had planted overturned on the sidewalk. Two other officers stood a few feet away from Alicia, shielding their eyes from the sun. "There," one said to the other, and pointed to the small attic window. Squinting, Alicia caught a flash of Palmer's maroon hat. She wouldn't have believed she'd seen him if not for the policemen pointing. She grabbed Louise's other arm and squeezed hard, bruising her fingers into her mother's skin, harder than was necessary.

Louise twisted free of Alicia's grip. "What are you doing?" Louise's cheeks had reddened and she looked at Alicia like she might slap her, something she had never done. Alicia almost wanted her to.

"Up there," Alicia said, pointing. "He's up there," she said again, though she had intended to say something else, to explain.

Louise squinted at the attic window, her lips parted in an agitated grimace. One of the officers began to speak to them then, explaining how Palmer had been shot in the foot when a policeman had tried to disarm him and how he'd retreated to the attic and locked himself in. Louise pulled her freed wrist close to her chest, and then she seemed to draw into herself, as if now that she knew Palmer was alive, she was finished with caring.

Alicia tried to reach for her, but Louise shook off the gesture, turning only to make eye contact before she moved back toward the car.

"Wait," Alicia said, but she knew her mother wouldn't hear her.

Alicia froze for a moment, her weight shifted toward her mother, and then she stopped. Maybe Louise's strange behavior all through the months with Palmer had been just disinterested curiosity at a new species of man, and not love, like Alicia now had to admit she'd hoped. Glancing over her shoulder at Louise, who was fetching her driving shoes from the trunk, she suddenly thought that being a detached researcher tracing the path of her mother's life seemed unkind. But not just unkind. Also unsatisfactory. And that was when she understood that she, Alicia, a separate person from her mother, was the one who'd grown to care so much for Palmer. It was love she felt, not romantic love, something deeper than that.

She began to move across the yard, gingerly at first, past the two conspiring officers, who somehow didn't stop her, and then faster, toward the house's entrance. She put her foot on the front step, and then one of the officers was there. "No," he said. "You can't do that. That's an unstable man in there." He took her roughly by the shoulder.

But Alicia slid from under his hands and darted back out onto the lawn, to where she could see the attic window. She heard the policeman's shouts, the garble of squad car radios, the neighbors across the street calling out, their voices strangely soft, like crickets. "Palmer?" she called.

Some shuffling and unsteady movement and Palmer's head emerged from the window, the maroon ball cap, his face pale. "Alicia?" he said. He looked nervously at the police officers frozen in the yard, their hands hovering above their gun holsters.

And then, as if it were something unstoppable, the Southern migration of birds or the equinox, Alicia's voice spiraled up to him. She told him about Jim and the interview, about the fancy hotel and the clip-winged parrots and the ice sculptures and the designer luggage. And while she talked, she thought how Ms. Hastings was right about magic, how true magic was much simpler than the kind Louise had been looking for all these years. It came from the real world, from moving into a place and unpacking and really living there, from talking to a real man in a real attic to stop the worst real thing from happening. "Come down and talk to me," she told Palmer. "I promise it's going to be okay. Come down and let me in."

Mad Dog

At that moment three years ago when John Casey had signed up for University Challenge, he could not have known that the BBC cameras would love him, that the incongruity of his Washington Senators baseball cap, his impossibly swift answers to questions from any academic field, and his penchant for the exclamation "Who da brain man!" would make him a stand-out on the Lancaster University team. He had no way of guessing that tossing his head back and howling after each correct answer, something he started on a total whim and then continued even after he had been scolded and told to stop, would earn him the status of nationally adored rapscallion (John "Mad Dog" Casey).

After all, the real John Casey was just an egghead foreign exchange student, a homesick, small-town Virginia boy with the musical talent to be a concert pianist, the first Casey to go to college instead of right into the Toyota dealership off the southbound I-66 Smoky Ordinary exit. His family, which had lived in Smoky Ordinary for five generations, actually owned the elephant in the local TV ads, the one on which Grandpa Red perched when he shouted his message about ten tons of terrific Toyotas.

"This will all be yours," Grandpa used to whisper to John when all of the other cousins were outside playing football and the two of them were at the piano bench. Then he would gesture to a framed photograph of the elephant with a distant, misty admiration. "You're the only one who's as smart as Bessie." But, as it turned out, the future had other plans for John Casey.

At first, as the acclaim grew, and as John grew into his Mad Dog persona, everything had seemed fan-freaking-tastic—there was an exclusive interview in *The Sun*, an appearance on *This Morning*, four months later a ghost-written autobiography (*Mad Dog*), and two months after that a top 20 CD featuring him on piano and primal wail (*Mad Dog*). There was a particular A-list London party during which he snuck into an upstairs parlor to play Rachmaninoff's piano concerto number three in D minor on a baby grand, and ended up impressing his favorite hip-hop artist, Suga Bear, who stood in the doorway and clapped when he finished. Since then, the two of them had become friends, real friends who talked about music, art, the hassles of fame; it was like something from his dreams.

And the money. God, the money. His accountant made him buy stuff, property and the like, just so he could keep some of that money busy.

Now, though, he understood that he was trapped on this island by his own condition as a minor celebrity. He'd had his fifteen minutes, a backlash was forming, the US populace hadn't the faintest idea who he was, and the UK was the only place where the term "comeback" was going to make any sense. Only, when he did come back, he was determined to be known this time for what he was. He was not just some idiot savant pop-singing redneck here for the amusement of know-nothings who bought *The Sun* and ogled the topless girl on Page Three. He was not what that critic in *The London Review of Books* said last week—"the clearest indication of a people beset by the tremulous urge to crawl back into the trees and communicate via guttural emissions from whatever aperture is most convenient." He was in MENSA; he held degrees in music and European history from UVA; his professors had assured him that his abilities as a pianist could afford him a professional standing.

In order to reinvent himself, he just needed a bit of preparation. At his first acting lesson, last week, his coach told him he had potential. With his wholesome everyman looks and his natural ability to feel the words as he spoke them, he could be a Brando or a Dean—if he could re-direct himself. Instead of bursting out everywhere, like a ray of sunshine, he should be a charcoal briquette, still and maybe even grey on the outside, pulsing hot within. He wasn't sure he wanted to be enigmatic like that, though. He hadn't enrolled in the class because he wanted to become an actor, but rather in order to learn how to project the person he felt he actually was on the inside.

So, no matter how his publicist begged him, he would not howl. Not now, not ever again. The howling had become forced in recent months anyway, something he did because someone pointed at a camera and said do it. There was no emotion in it now. It made him feel like someone waking up on the floor the morning after a party, realizing that prancing around with the hostess's pantyhose on his head had been hilarious only while it was happening, and then mainly to himself.

He refused to miss his mother and his father and his brothers and cousins back in Smoky Ordinary, Virginia, or to dwell on the fact that everyone back home saw his enthusiastic nature as a good thing ("Full of the joys of spring, that boy") and never as a lack of finesse, the way people did here. It was true that the people who knew him best were easily fooled by a forced positive attitude. Back home, if he grinned and had a strong handshake, everyone would assume he was a perfect example of virtue. No one back home had a shit detector, that was for sure. But he preferred this positivity to the European philosophy on life, which as far as he could tell was, Everything sucks. And yes, this includes you, loser.

His growing anger toward his decidedly B-list girlfriend helped him to stay strong, to stay focussed on recovery, on climbing to the top, far away from her. She was right now, in fact, nagging him about his dog, Stevie—droning on and on in an accent that some time ago he had stopped finding quaint or charming.

There were two things he would not do in response to her annoying complaints. First, he would not wrestle her to the floor and tickle her until she wet her pants or had sex with him. That had gotten old. And second, he would not pick up the nearest item that belonged to her, in this case a Ted Baker handbag, and throw it out the living room window. He wasn't there yet. The urge to do something dramatic was just an itch in his stomach, an itch he could hold inside him.

"It's not your fault," said John to Stevie, who had left a trail of paw prints on the dining room chairs; Stevie was small for a black Labrador, and had the habit of hopping onto furniture to make himself more imposing. "You're a beautiful animal and you can get on the table any time you feel like it," John said. He scraped some dirt off a dining room chair with a still-sealed letter from his publicist, Ian Hawthornthwaite. Letters from Ian gave John the urge to go home, but still he refused to miss Mexican food and Reese's Peanut Butter Cups and Thanksgiving and the Fourth of July. He refused to miss Bunny O'Connor's annual Barbeque Wing-Ding out on her farm. He absolutely refused to miss Amber, his younger sister by eleven months, his closest friend in the world, so much like him they nearly shared a photographic, 140 IQ brain.

Amber, who was brimming with her first pregnancy, had called him just yesterday and eagerly told him, laughing, that she could no longer see her feet, even when she bent over. "I tell you, this kid eats all my food, stays up all hours. He's a bad influence on me. Come to think of it, he's just like you." Her voice dropped to a whisper. "God, I swear my flatulence sounds like that awful thing you used to do, when you would toot the opening notes of Watermusik. Remember?"

57

Of course he remembered. It was the nature of the brains they had to remember everything—and to suck up information wherever they found it. He remembered the two of them lying side-by-side on their stomachs in front of the fireplace when they were nine and ten years old, reading together each volume from the set of encyclopedias their dad had worked overtime to buy; it had taken John and Amber two years to read all of those burgundy books. He could still feel their heft, the rough faux-leather covers, the raised gold lettering. The books were exotic to him, both in their appearance and content, as if they were erudite French men who had taken up residence in the Caseys' brown and tan wood-panelled living room, making it their café, smoking impossibly potent cigarettes and rolling ideas back and forth between them with the kind of passion that in this part of Virginia was reserved only for football.

He could see his younger brother Jason's tight, worried face, when he and Amber forced him to play the host for "Encyclopedia Jeopardy," a game they invented to test what they had absorbed. Amber had won half their contests, but it hadn't been enough for her; she had been a sore loser when she wasn't the quickest to answer, and punished herself. One time she had snatched the notes from poor little Jason's sweaty hand, stuffed the paper into her mouth, and eaten it in an exaggerated fashion, like a cow, her little fruit-shaped nose rotating with the effort. She often pressed her fingers to her forehead when she couldn't solve a puzzle, as if she might be able to physically manipulate the contents of her thoughts.

John refused to imagine the dramatic curve of her abdomen, a curve he would never see himself. She would have her baby any day now, and given that the television event that would change his public image—somehow, he just didn't know how—would arrive in just two nights, turning his life upside down all over again, thoughts of jumping on a plane for home in time to see her pregnant were entirely wasteful. Even if he wasn't planning something big, he was contractually obligated to do the stupid show, as Ian had pointed out, none too gently, the other day.

His girlfriend, Vivian, looked up now from her lunch and glared at the dog. "Not his fault that our carpet looks like a muddy farmyard? Yes, it bloody well is his fault. Or no, actually it's your fucking fault for letting the little shite in the house." She flicked her two-toned hair over her shoulder. "The little sod has tracked grass and dirt all over the room. I think it's in my food."

"Grass would probably have more nutritional value than that thing you're eating. Watercress and bread is not a sandwich," John said calmly. "Just so you know."

Vivian's forehead wrinkled with confusion. She squinted.

His normal response to her was a bit less straightforward, a bit more jovial, something like "Shaddap, Luv" in a bad imitation of her accent. He had realized early on that intelligent conversation with Vivian was all but impossible. They engaged in verbal combat instead, like a foreign language comprised entirely of swear words. But now that he'd disengaged from it, taken one of the first steps toward the new persona he would adopt, he saw too clearly how awful it was.

"Don't be a twat, John," she said now. "It's time for you to behave. There are only three days left." Then she smiled, far too broadly to be authentic, and threw the so-called sandwich at him.

John ducked, the sandwich distributed its contents across the carpet, and Stevie darted out from under the table and scarfed everything up. He belched and looked at John, as if wondering what might come next. Would the crazy woman start giving him all her food now?

Vivian wasn't finished. "Three days!" she shrieked. She coughed and clutched at her throat. "Uch," she said, and stuck her fingers into her mouth, pulling out limp strands of what looked to be grass. "I know what's going on," she said. "I can tell you're out to sabotage me. You don't care about Saturday night, you selfish prick."

"Don't waste all your dramatics on me, darlin'," he said. John knew Vivian could weep at the snap of her own sparkly, manicured fingers. She often did it in the presence of reporters in order to get closer to the front page. "Save it for the cameras. And don't forget, Miss Potty Mouth, when you get up there and start acting like a fool, it's live television. You screw up, you'll be right back where you started, giving perms to grandmas."

Vivian, formerly a humble hairdresser, was a finalist on *Pop Idol*. Ian Hawthornethwaite had already made a deal with the show's producers for her to be named the winner, on the condition that John would be permitted to rush the stage in an apparent burst of spontaneous emotion. He was supposed to howl, which John had said was out of the question. "I'm over that," he'd told Ian. "I'm not going to leave my seat."

"Oh, I'm afraid you will, sweetheart," Ian had said to him with an air of menace that John had never heard before. Ian was a five foot eight, slim gay man, normally jolly and fabulous, but at that moment, the glint in his eye was a clear view of something ruthless—like a tornado swirling above, not yet touching down but threatening to, its scorpion tail poised for a precise strike.

"You've been up your own crack hole all week," Vivian said to him now. "You better not skive on Saturday."

"Oh, I'll be there. Don't you worry." He gave her a knowing look, as if he had a plan. He wanted a plan, but for now, he did not have anything like one.

Ian had hooked John up with Vivian a few months earlier, when she made her initial tanned and busty appearance on the promotional preview for this season's *Pop Idol.* For him, it was a simple mathematical equation—two B-list celebrities in an interesting-enough relationship equalled an exponential leap onto the A list. He insisted that they be seen together at clubs in London and for long weekends here at John's house in the Lake District. John and Vivian didn't really hit it off, to say the very least. She hated the country and said his four bedroom stone cottage with the Lake Windermere view was "like a morgue or some-fink." She paced, she sat on the floor with her head in her hands, she drank Lambrini straight from the bottle, she phoned friends down south and spoke in Cockney rhyming slang even though she wasn't originally from London, she went through John's clothes and threw away everything that wasn't Paul Smith or Dolce & Gubana, everything that he'd snuck into his wardrobe since her last visit. She refused to acknowledge the expanse of emerald hills that stretched to the horizon in every direction or the way that they cupped the water of the lake between them or the way the light could change the color palette from greens to blues to grays and back again.

As near as he could tell, she was only happy when she was in London and wearing pink plastic pants and walking down the street speaking loudly to her friends on the phone about how expensive the pink plastic pants were. The only thing worse was when the friends were actually present, and she was drinking bottles of blue WKD, and, eventually on all fours in the plastic pants vomiting in a side alley, John shuddered just thinking about this.

"That's the charm of it, love," Ian liked to say, caressing his own pencil-thin gray mustache. "Don't think Stupid bitchy cow." And here he would hold up his palms in a theatrical manner. "Think instead Hot. Volatile." A few weeks ago, Ian had laid out the plan for John to propose to Vivian. It was to happen tomorrow, down in London, on the sidewalk in front of Toni & Guy, the haircutting chain from which Vivian had been rescued by her *Pop Idol* stardom. John had reluctantly agreed to do it. He thought now the proposal was probably going to be a mistake, even though it wouldn't be for real. Call him old fashioned for thinking it, maybe, but John and Vivian just didn't have much in common. The extent of their relationship had been having some very interesting sex involving devices and orifices he had never fully explored before. No complaints on that count, of course, but there wasn't much beyond it.

Ian's guidance was all John had known of show business, and Ian was leading John toward a tabloid engagement despite his misgivings. At this point, the only person John knew who might be able to help him was Suga Bear. Even if Suga Bear couldn't think of a way to get John out of Vivian and Ian's clutches, maybe he would have a way of making the whole situation not seem so terribly crass.

Ian had leased a, like, billion carat diamond ring, which now lay in a plastic bag on the kitchen floor, where Vivian had thrown it during her most recent outburst this morning. "Hideous piece of shite! It's not even gold!" she had said. She hollered more than any girl John had ever met. And when she did, her voice was deep and lusty as if she were a life-long smoker, which in fact she was. Smokers, as it turned out, had a lot of financial cache in Britain, and in Vivian (or "Viv" as she was lovingly known), they had found their champion—a long-legged, gap-toothed hairdresser from Kent with a gift for the harmonica and low-cut satin tops, a devotion to smoking that bordered on religious. She was now in talks with both Marlboro and Camel.

"It's platinum," John had informed her about the ring. "You know? The malleable metallic element? Atomic weight 195.08. Very valuable." And then, almost as if he couldn't help himself: "But if you had any class, you'd probably know that."

Before John knew what was happening, she had taken off her 80s style pump and swatted him in the arm with the pointed heel. He'd been proud of himself; he hadn't responded. Now, five hours later, he bore a large sore welt there and his arm felt weak. He rubbed the bump, and in spite of a dark look from Vivian, slid onto the floor and sat with the dog instead of at the table. Probably, he thought, there were a lot of men who liked their dogs more than their girlfriends.

A few months ago, Ian had wrangled John a gig as the main spokesperson for the Royal Society for the Prevention of Cruelty to Animals, on the condition that John himself would adopt a dog. The whole thing had seemed like it would be easy enough, because he liked pets. Back home in Smoky Ordinary, his mother and father kept chickens, homing

pigeons, and bees—all of which had a tranquil, soothing sort of presence when you were standing out in the back pasture listening to them
and to the faraway hum of traffic on I-66. But nothing inside of John
had prepared him for posing for magazine ads with scarred, burnt, and
hairless puppies, with one-eyed cats, or with the pony that had the razor
blades lodged permanently in its neck. Sometimes he sat bolt upright
in bed, gasping.

These days, he thought of Stevie as being more human than most
people he knew. The dog was familiar. He responded to John's voice in
ways John expected. This was more than he could say about most English people, who assumed, just because he had an American accent, that
he must be unusually slim, that his intelligence was some kind of genet-
ic anomaly, that he had developed a sense of humor only after his arrival
on British soil, and that he would be completely fulfilled as soon as he
could find the time to finish that genealogical study of his Irish roots. At
the end of each day, the dog waited for him at the living room window,
studying each car, each person. When he spotted John he jumped off
the sofa, and a blur of wagging tail disappeared from the frame of the
window. Then the dog would be waiting to greet him inside the front
door, leaping and licking. On some days, John did experiments to see at
what range the dog could recognize him. He waved his arms as he approached the house or he said, "It's me" in a variety of different voices.
The truth was, though, that Stevie had usually clocked him long before
he ever clocked Stevie. This ritual of theirs—that hopeful stare and
the outline of those slightly lopsided ears—was one of the only things
in John's life that made him grin completely unconsciously. He was
so surprised to realize he was grinning that he sometimes covered his
mouth like a little kid.

Vivian now glowered at John from where she sat at the table. Then
the creepy smile returned to her face. She picked up a rubber ball and,
with surprising accuracy, tossed it down the hall into the bathroom. The
dog went skidding after it, panting, huge pink tongue flapping happily
to one side. Vivian dashed from her chair chased the dog, cornering
him in the bathroom. "Sucker," she said in a terrible imitation of John's
accent, and then she shut the dog in there with the light off. She kicked
the door once with her bare foot, and John heard Stevie yelp.

Stevie was a rescue dog. At this very moment, there was a photograph of John (Mad Dog) and Stevie plastered on the outsides of city
busses throughout the country. The slogan read: "One of these dogs
was chained in a dark cellar for two years. How mad is that?" The

fine print explained that the RSPCA had put Stevie through rehabilitation so that he could walk, run, navigate ordinary sidewalks, and live without fear. This last item, strictly speaking, hadn't been a complete success, as Stevie had a variety of paralyzing phobias associated with things like trashcans, statues, men in uniforms, curbs, and enclosed dark spaces. He now began shrieking and scratching at the bathroom door. John thought of the dog as something like his uncle, Frank, who'd been to Vietnam, someone with trapdoors in his mind, someone who had to avoid fear the way some people had to avoid shellfish.

"You are one cold bitch," John said to Vivian, as he strode to the bathroom and released Stevie. The dog darted between John's legs and peed on the Persian rug in the front hall, something he hadn't done in a record-breaking three weeks. The dog's ears were back and his tail limp, and he was looking at John with a bewildered expression a person might have after being mugged. John could almost see a question mark forming in the wet glint of Stevie's dark eyes, in the wrinkles of the dog's forehead. How could she? And how could you let her? he seemed to be saying. John opened his mouth, as if he might be able to explain things, but of course what explanation could there be for what she'd just done? With no answer forthcoming, Stevie trotted into the living room, tail between his legs, and crawled into the small space between the couch and the wall. John could see him curled up into a tight ball, shivering.

The dog wouldn't come out for probably an hour. Unless, of course, John were to howl. Whenever he did this, the dog's face became slack and peaceful, eyes half-closed, the same look that came over some people's faces when they listened to Miles Davis. After a few moments, the dog's beautiful black muzzle rounded to a sweet perfect "o" almost like he was going to blow a smoke ring toward the ceiling. And then, eventually, he let out a mournful howl of his own, such a sad sound that it reminded John not of Miles Davis, but of an opera singer, of Maria Callas, a noise of true tragedy. But he couldn't do this now. He couldn't howl. He couldn't give Vivian the satisfaction. "That's just fucking great," John said and smacked the wall just above Vivian's shoulder. She was tall for a British girl, but John's six feet and one inch made him a giant here. Still, she didn't so much as flinch. John closed his eyes for a moment and composed himself. Her face was only inches from his. "You know, I could imagine a despot like you taking over a small country," he said.

"Yeah, Britain," she said, grinning. "That's the plan." Her voice. That gap-toothed grin. She was so fucking sexy. But he hated her. Suga

Flann

Bear hated her. His family would probably hate her (though they would never say so and would offer her gallons of iced tea and potato salad to assuage their guilt). He needed to remember this, he thought, glancing down at the crack of her supple, tanned cleavage. Sometimes lately, John felt as though he was drifting. In spite of his remarkable memory, his overall perception of his home in Virginia had become sketchy, a place from a dream he could not quite recall. And yet England, even though he was in it, seemed equally fuzzy—celebrities he'd never heard of, foods too bland to register on his American taste buds, an endless number of slang expressions that he didn't understand. "Don't you go pickin' up anymore of that funny accent, Jack," his mother had said on the phone the other day when he'd referred to what he was wearing as a "jumper" rather than a sweater. He hadn't even realized he'd done it and he'd felt weird, like when he'd heard his own CD for the first time—like he was outside himself, like he was two different Johns at the same time.

But this. He looked at Vivian, the adorable upturn of her too-broad nose. This here was something concrete, something he could hold onto; his hands tingled, imagining touching Vivian's bare skin, the mole inside her right thigh. He hated her, and somehow sleeping with her was the only thing that distracted him from this fact. He wanted to stop feeling homesick, picturing Amber's big, wholesome belly and the whole family gathered around her in the hospital.

What can it hurt? he thought now. What difference does it make? He nuzzled into Vivian's neck, which smelled like coconut, nothing like the floral woodsy scent of the few girls he'd known back home. He inhaled sharply, involuntarily. This was good. This was good. This was too good. He gripped her silky hair in his fists.

"Bite me, Mad Dog," she breathed in his ear. "Bite me hard."

"So you're engaged, huh, boy?" Suga Bear grinned behind his dark glasses and gestured to page five of *The Daily Mirror* on the table. Suga had taken a detour through London to see his wife and kids and also to see John; he'd asked John to meet him at Café Nero near King's Cross. His ultimate destination was Newcastle, one of the stops on his Gold N Delicious European Tour. Stevie perked up when he recognized Suga's voice, bounding toward the singer, nuzzling the hems of his oversized shorts and licking the large gold Suga ring on his left hand.

"Have a seat," Suga said to John, gesturing to the chair across from him. It was one of those rare sunny days in England, when the sky was blue and cloudless, and you could actually sit at the outdoor tables on the narrow pedestrian streets and wear short sleeves and sip coffee and pretend you were in a temperate part of Europe, where the produce was fresh, and people didn't rage against the darkness by binge drinking and punching each other in the face. John sat down and closed his eyes for a moment and listened to women's shoes echoing on the cobblestones. As Suga patted Stevie and spoke softly to him, he reached out his other hand and pushed the newspaper toward John's side of the table. "I proposed to my wife on a long walk in Kensington Gardens," Suga said. "Lots of songbirds, some pigeons. No cameras."

John didn't want to see that picture again—he and Vivian kissing. He hated pictures of himself anyway, the way his nose and chin looked so pointy when he smiled and the way his thick sandy hair was always messed up, as if he were the only person on earth to be followed perpetually by a gust of wind. But this one nearly brought him to his knees when he saw it this morning. The photographer had caught them finishing their kiss. John's brow was deeply furrowed and his eyes were half-lidded, like someone having a seizure. Vivian's face was all bliss, all relaxation, except for her tongue, which was just visible between their two mouths. The flash had caused a string of saliva to glisten. "My mother's going to kill me when she finds out," John said. He folded the paper in half. "I guess I can hope she never sees it, right?"

Suga laughed. "Whatever you say, Dog."

John felt his face get hot. Suga didn't need to remind him that he, Suga, had never engaged in publicity stunts. His six number one songs spoke for themselves. If only John hadn't cut that vapid pop album two years ago. How had he let it get this far? "This is the last thing I do for Ian and Vivian. I mean it."

Now Stevie let out a big sigh, turned around several times, and lay down heavily on Suga's foot. John gazed at the dog, noting with some pride how much progress he was making. Stevie bristled a little when Rupert, Suga's new bodyguard, rushed over to the table with a bag from The Body Shop. Rupert was a six-foot-five British-born Jamaican, whose footfalls were always audible. But even though Rupert was a stranger, and a big one, Stevie didn't nip Rupert's feet and he didn't have a fear-induced pee under the table. Rupert tore the top off the packaging and lifted out a translucent plastic bottle. "They're having a sale on bath oil. You want me to get you some?"

"No, but get me a newspaper, will you?" Suga said to Rupert. "A real one. I mean it, not that crappy one with the naked chick inside." He tossed Rupert a two-pound coin. Rupert fumbled it and had to crawl under some neighboring tables.

"Bath oil?" John said, grinning.

"Don't laugh," Suga whispered. He checked that Rupert wasn't listening. "He doesn't have a sense of humor."

John nodded.

"Anyway, I have some news for you," Suga said. He put down his coffee. "I spoke to Barry."

"Barry, really?" Barry was a junior executive at Suga's record company. John had met him at a party once. He wore a designer suit and gold hoop earrings. He looked like he was about twenty-five, about the same age as John. They were a lot alike, except that Barry had the quietly cocky, generous spirit of somebody who had everything figured out, and you could tell he would end up making more money than any of the musicians he signed.

"Yeah, yeah. Straight up. Barry says the whole image change concept thing sounds, well, okay." Then Suga made quotation marks with his fingers. "In theory."

"That doesn't sound very promising."

"Well, he said historically it doesn't happen all that often, and I asked him what that meant, and then he rattled off all these numbers. Basically he just said a bunch of crap we already know: It's hard to appeal to people who don't know you exist, and it's a little harder to appeal to people who maybe wish you didn't." Suga threw his hands up.

"Oh," John said, disappointed.

"Look, just forget all that shit," Suga said. "There's a better long-range plan for a guy like you. Just be yourself instead of Ian's monkey boy."

"You really think so?" It was what he wanted to do, desperately. Maybe John had just wanted to hear someone else say it.

"I was thinking maybe you and I could work on a project together."

"You're joking, right?"

"Nah. I've got a jazz/hip hop fusion kind of thing in mind. Don't tell anyone, but I've been listening to Diana Krall. Very grown up." Suga pushed a disc across the table. "Listen to this and let me know what you think we can do with it."

Suga really seemed to enjoy helping John, though sometimes John wondered why. They weren't in the same league. Maybe it was payback, a gentleman's gratitude after John had contributed some of the more complicated arrangements on Suga's latest album, particularly the Bess Armstrong samples in a song about a real-life murdered teenaged prostitute from the east end of London, someone Suga believed the TV news had forgotten about.

66

John picked up the CD. "Yeah, okay," he said, pulling a small spiral notebook from his back pocket and jotting a few notes.

"Trust me," Suga said, gesturing again to the newspaper. "Soon you won't need this crap." He dipped his head and looked over his glasses for a moment at the paper. "You really need to lose these fools you're with now. Ian Hawthornethwaite would sell his left nut if the price was right. Vivian would sell her nuts, for that matter. And she might sell yours, too."

John nodded. He hoped Suga was right about finally leaving the absurdity behind. Even though it had been fake, the proposal had had a deep impact on him. Vivian had, of course, wept like a beauty queen, and the reporters Ian had phoned attracted a crowd of a hundred or so curious passersby, who shouted encouragement to John while he was down on one knee and choking out his words. His hands shaking and his voice cracking, he'd been on the verge of actual tears, and for a whole day since. He kept thinking about the life he would have had if he hadn't gone away to UVA and then to England, if he'd stayed near home like Amber and gone to Georgetown and then gotten married for real.

What if he'd never left Smoky Ordinary? He could picture college, working weekends and summers with his older brothers at the Toyota dealership. Honest work—or at least as honest as selling cars ever got. And now, a few years later, he could imagine the little brick ranch house he and his wife would have (he was sure he would have a wife, someone local named Amy or Tonia or Stacy)—there would be azaleas, porkchop dinners, and plenty of wicker. A stream behind the house, the banks thick with blackberry bushes he would cheerfully fight year-round. A baby grand piano in the sitting room, where he would play when his wife's friends and their husbands came over, surprising the men and impressing the women.

He wouldn't have missed the last few years of Bunny O'Connor's annual barbecues on her farm. He and the wife, along with Amber and her husband, Cal, would have attended every one, loading up on potato salad and cornbread, getting comfortably fat, promising to go for a jog the next morning, reminiscing about how, when they were kids, they used to play underneath the stage. People around them would talk about poor Joe Hawksworth, who had fallen off the town water tower and been impaled on his own car antenna. Or about the way Grandpa Red was sweet on old Bunny, coaxing her to ride with him on the elephant down Market Street, past the P&W's Eatery and Pink's Tiny Pink Grocery—even though no one else was allowed even to touch Bessie, ever.

But John and the wife and Amber and Cal wouldn't take much notice. Stevie would sit at their feet, somehow Stevie would be there, and they would watch the entertainment, several badly dressed guys playing steel guitars and dulcimers. And maybe, just maybe, if he were still in Smoky Ordinary, he would have made something of himself, too. He would be known for something other than a stupid noise humans weren't supposed to make.

"Do you ever miss home?" John said to Suga. "Don't you miss your hometown?"

Suga took his dark glasses off, put them on the table, and squinted. His brown eyes were enormous, with long, soft eyelashes. "Look at me," Suga said. "I'm a half-Vietnamese, half-black man who grew up in bum-fuck North Carolina. Those people couldn't even pronounce my name. I ended up being called Wang, because it was as close as they could get. No, I don't miss it, Dog." He paused and then gestured over his shoulder. "Why you think I moved to London, when I could live anywhere in the world? No one here ever treats my kids like ghetto trash. These Brits—most of them anyway—got over all that a long time ago."

John studied Suga for a long moment. It had never occurred to him in any meaningful way that Suga was black or that he was Vietnamese or anything else. Suga was just Suga. He puzzled over this for a moment and then he moved on. "So then what about the show tomorrow night?" he said.

Suga looked over John's shoulder at Rupert, who was returning with the newspaper. "All right, here's the deal. Rupert and me, we're going to go with you to the show. All three of us, shades on, cool and calm. We slip out of there the second Vivian finishes." Suga smiled.

Attending a show like *Pop Idol* was so far beneath Suga, it wasn't even funny. Suga's own publicist would probably burst a gasket. "Thanks," John said. "Really. I owe you."

"Yeah, everybody'll be talking about it. They'll know something's up. Think of it as early PR for our record."

John frowned, becoming aware that Rupert had managed to wedge himself under the table with the dog, whose tail was slapping against John's leg with each wag. Rupert was rubbing Stevie's belly. Stevie was sprawled out on the pavement, and it looked for all the world like he was smiling.

"This dog is wicked," Rupert said.

Suga unfolded *The Sun*. "I said no naked chicks," he said.

"I don't know what you're on about. Who doesn't like naked chicks?"

Suga rolled his eyes. "Yeah, that's right. I forgot."

"Hey, Rupert, I get you—naked chicks probably use lots of bath oil," John said. "What's not to like?" Actually, he could think of plenty of things. The very sight of *The Sun* caused a hot anger to creep up his guts and into his neck. "I mean, so what if the language is at an eight-year-old reading level? So what if it's only something a complete wanker would buy?"

From under the table, Rupert's hand seized John's balls with surprising accuracy.

John gasped.

"I let it go the first time, didn't I?" Rupert said from under the table. "At least I make an effort, don't I? I bet you don't even read poetry to your lady."

"Derek Walcott," John said, breathless, hoping Rupert wouldn't squeeze. "West Indies. Nobel Laureate, 1992."

"Hmm." He let go and then he crawled out from under the table. "I prefer Tennyson myself." John exhaled.

"Well, back when I had a copy of *The Guardian*," Suga was saying, looking almost through John, seemingly oblivious to what had just occurred, speaking about *The Guardian* as if it were a girl he used to know. "I saw a survey of school children about what they want to be when they grow up. Ninety percent of them said they wanted to be famous. Do you know what they wanted to be famous for?"

"What?"

Suga leaned across the table and grabbed John's arm. "They had no fucking idea."

Rupert unfolded himself and rose to his full height. With something like fondness, he patted John on the shoulder with his enormous hand. John tried not to flinch. "That's just it," John said, forcing his gaze back to Suga. "Why am I famous? What the hell have I ever done?"

"That's all about to change, son. You've got skills," Suga said, pointing emphatically at his own head.

A couple of adolescent girls, wobbly in high-heeled boots, approached and stood behind Suga, giggling. Suga signed his name on a napkin. They clutched it and ran off like squirrels, like the squirrels that used to raid the bird feeder back home. Of course, there weren't any squirrels in British cities, not even in the parks. But John refused to miss them now, when he thought about it. It would be weird to miss squirrels.

"Think about it, Dog. There isn't a reason you're famous. Nobody deserves this," Suga said, gesturing to the girls. "Nobody deserves to be treated like a god." Suga had his hands laced together on top of the tabloid and he was staring at John.

"I know, I know," John said. Sometimes, he thought, Suga got impossibly deep and virtuous, like the Dalai Lama, or Jesus: no porn, no drug arrests, no unearned acclaim.

"But it's not about you," Suga continued. "It's about them. They don't know it, maybe, but they need someone who's about more than instant gratification."

"Vivian has her moments, though," John blurted out. The other night, up at Windermere, she'd pressed her naked body against the floor-to-ceiling window in his bedroom and let the reporter hiding in the bushes snap away. He'd laughed until tears streamed down his face. Suga was right—she had balls, that girl. Compared to her, he wasn't sure he had the stomach for this business. "And then, sometimes, I want to go back home," John said.

"You will." Suga smiled. "You can, that is, if you want to. You've got the freedom to do just about anything you want. You've got something that ninety percent of people don't. And that they haven't realized they need. Talent."

Squirrels, pregnant sisters, summertime barbecues, Toyotas: They all sounded good. John was pretty sure he wanted to go home. But then, sometimes, he could picture himself and Vivian in an English country house doing English country things like traipsing around in Wellies with Stevie and eating heavy desserts involving spongecake and custard. Of course, he always pictured this as if it were a TV show, not real life. In real life, Vivian exposed herself to strangers and in the morning got mad at John and put his underwear down the garbage disposal—a disposal he'd had imported because British houses didn't have them.

"You can do better than all this exhibitionist crap," Suga said, sighing. "Get rid of Ian and we'll do this CD. It could blow up, and I mean big. US markets. Everything."

Get rid of Ian? It sounded so complicated. It sounded like something that would involve attorneys and nineteen months of negotiations. John didn't know if he could wait. He was thinking about what he could sell—maybe all that stuff Ian made him buy, the Porsche he never drove, the house in Spain he'd visited once. The money could keep him and Amy or Tonia or Stacy going for some time, even at the current US rate of exchange. He could picture arriving at Dulles Airport with Stevie, no photographers there to greet him, no one shouting, "Mad Dog, look over here!" Mad Dog would be no more. There would only be the quiet of family and black nights with stars.

"I can't fire Ian. He's under contract, and I'd have to pay him just about everything I've got."

Rupert snorted, muttered under his breath. "Barmy."

"What?" John said.

"Fuckin' hell," the bodyguard grumbled. "Publicists get fired every day. Even I know that. Who explained your contract to you? Ian?" Rupert turned, waved a hand at John in disgust, and stormed off. "For a bright bloke, you really are daft," he said over his shoulder.

John's mouth hung open for a moment, and then he and Suga looked at each other and started to laugh. "He's said more words today than he has in the whole three months he's worked for me." Suga shook his head with something like awe. "I think he likes you."

The next day, the day of the show, Vivian woke up in their London hotel room with a cold. She refused to come out of their bathroom and was still in there when Ian came by.

"Don't worry, luv," Ian said to the locked door. "You're known for your husky voice. Just work it."

"Work it?" she said. "Listen to me. I sound like Bart Simpson. Where's John?"

"I'm here," John said.

Vivian opened the door. Her skin was blotchy and her eyes watered. She had on a fluffy white bathrobe and bunny slippers. Without make-up, she looked like a woman at her toilette in an Edgar Degas pastel, her skin as fine as rice paper. Then the stats rolled through John's mind. Edgar Degas: Impressionist, France, 1834-1917. "What should I do?" she said to John.

She had never asked his advice before. About anything. "Let's hear you sing," he said. She belted out a few lines of her song, Anastasia's "Set Me Free." It sounded fine, just like all the other million times he'd heard her sing it in his house. But just before she got to the chorus, she sputtered and coughed, doubling over as if she might be sick. "I'm buggered," she croaked.

"Don't worry," Ian said, already dialling his mobile phone. "It's not typhoid. Or Ebola. There's a doctor who owes me. He's been shagging a certain famous someone and they want it kept quiet." He winked and then he plugged his other ear with his finger and walked away from them.

John realized that his hand was on Vivian's back, so he gave her a gentle pat. She leaned into him. "What am I going to do, John?" she said. "I'm just a fucking hairdresser."

"Listen to me." He took her by the shoulders and looked right at her. "No, you're not."

He studied Vivian, the fear in her eyes. That was new. What had always made her different from other people, he thought, was her unwavering (oblivious?) belief that her best was most definitely good enough. He could see now for the first time ever a tiny bit of doubt. It softened the edges of her face, deepened her big aqua-blue eyes. She looked, well, pretty. "These doctors are very good," John said to her. He smiled. "They can cure laryngitis just like that." He snapped his fingers.

"Really?"

"You bet." John had no idea if what he'd said was true, but he genuinely wanted it to be. The depth of the feeling surprised him a little.

She produced a cigarette and a lighter from the pocket of her bathrobe. She gave John the lighter, her hand shaking, and put the cigarette to her lips. "Do the honors, will you, luv?"

When John got back from the corner shop with the bottle of cough syrup Ian's doctor suggested, Stevie wasn't in the hotel room. "Stevie?" he called. "Stevie?" He gently pushed on the bathroom door and it creaked open. There was no one there. His heart raced and he wandered around the hotel room for a moment patting his pockets, as if Stevie were a lost set of keys. Then, he found a note on the coffee table. We've taken the dog for a walk. He read it again and again. A walk? A walk? He tried to picture it, Ian and Vivian arm in arm strolling around Hyde Park with Stevie. But he couldn't. Neither of them had ever given two shits about the dog. They were both the kind of people who leaned away and withdrew their hands whenever the dog came near wagging his tail. Whenever, for some reason, they were forced to regard the dog, they screwed up their faces, as if they'd been presented with an enlarged photograph of bed mites.

No, this wasn't right. The one thing John knew for sure was that neither of them had any idea how to handle that dog. They would probably quite happily shut him in a suitcase and toss him in the trunk of a car.

John ran twenty blocks to the studio, picturing all of the ways Ian and Vivian might terrify Stevie—taking him past five-a-side soccer games, letting a German Shepherd too close, or even worse, riding in one of those noisy London black cabs. Was that who was really on Ian's phone –a cab driver? It was Friday afternoon, and he had to push past all of the

Mad Dog

people in black suits with briefcases, queuing at bus stops, reading paperback books. This was London, crowded, fast-paced, and silent—no honking, no talking. His lungs burned and he had to stop in a doorway and collect himself for a moment. He gulped for air. "Shit," he muttered. He could picture the confused wrinkles of the dog's forehead, the way a tooth sometimes caught on his lip when he was nervous, like a grimace. How could Stevie know if he was on his way to the park for a game of fetch or to a life trapped in a dark cellar? He wished he could scoop the dog into his arms. John saw the studio ahead and ignored the burning in his lungs. He dashed across a busy road. The light turned green and he had to zig-zag through the cars. When he finally got inside the building, gasping, he asked the receptionist for Vivian. Three large security guards stood in the entry way next to the desk.

"Sorry. She's not seeing anyone."

"Yeah, but I'm not just anyone," John said. Then he explained about the dog.

"They said you would say that," she said. "They said no exceptions."

"No exceptions, mate," said one of the security guards, who was now standing behind the receptionist with his arms folded across his chest.

"But the show starts in two hours. Your guest passes are here." She pushed them over the counter. "Perhaps you could pop down the road for a drink or something."

"Guest passes? A drink? Where's my fucking dog?"

"Not our problem, mate," said the man behind the counter.

"Jesus." John picked up the closest thing, which happened to be a pile of leaflets advertising *One Flew Over the Cuckoo's Nest* on the West End. He shook them in his hand and then flung them at the wall over the man's shoulder. A few of them hung in the air after the rest had fallen, fluttering down on the receptionist.

"See you later, mate," the security guard said tiredly, not moving. None of the people in the lobby moved, in fact, as if this sort of thing happened every day.

John went outside and called Suga. There was no answer; he left a message on Suga's voice mail. He leaned against the building and then slid down to the ground. He dialed his mother's number in Smoky Ordinary. When she answered, she was crying. He tried to pull himself together. "Mom, what is it?"

"Bunny O'Connor died this morning."

73

"Fuck me," John said slowly, letting the news wash over him. There was silence at the other end. "Bad language. Sorry, mom."

"They think it was a stroke."

"You okay?"

She sniffled. "Your brothers are here. We're going to bring a casserole over to the family in a few minutes. You want to say hi to Grandpa or Jason?" He could hear them talking in the background. He could picture them in the kitchen, bottles of root beer in their hands. He refused to miss root beer. "Where's Amber?" his mother said, her voice fainter as she turned away from the receiver. "Get Amber. Jack's on the phone." John could hear his brother Jason in the background explaining gently that Amber was in the hospital. "Yes, that's right. Of course she is ...." his mother said quietly.

"What? Has she had the baby?" John said. "Is she okay?"

There was a bunch of static on the line then. He could hear his mother's voice, but he couldn't make out any of the words. "Mom?" Nothing but more static, then a piercing electronic buzz. He jerked his head away and covered his ear. "Great!" he shouted. When several passersby turned to look at him, he stared them in the eye. "That's right, I'm mad! I'm a mad American sitting here on the sidewalk!"

He tried to call back several times, and then he let his hand fall to his lap and he pushed the button to disconnect.

Even the most critical of the judges could find little fault with Vivian's performance. As usual, she unwrapped a piece of Juicyfruit while they were talking to her and stood with her hip thrust to one side. She tilted her pretty honey-colored head and smiled. "Thank you. Oh, thank you very much," she said in response to their praise. Vivian always sounded sarcastic, even if she didn't mean to be.

In the audience, John, Suga and Rupert watched the proceedings. Suga took off his sunglasses, raised his eyebrows, and looked at John. "She doesn't seem sick to me."

"Oh, she's sick all right," John said. "She is one sick dog-stealing freak of nature."

With Rupert leading, John and Suga made their way through the crowd. The show wasn't over yet, and the complicated labyrinth of hallways backstage was relatively deserted. "Stevie, here boy," John called again and again, his voice echoing back to him from the cinderblock walls and metal doors. Rupert occasionally joined in. John paused and listened for Stevie. It gave him a chance to collect himself. He was afraid his voice would start to crack with desperation.

"How could you let them take your dog?" Rupert said, looking at John with real disdain.

"I didn't know they were going to take him, did I?"

"Never trust a publicist or a diva." Rupert turned and poked his finger into John's chest. "You are not in Kansas anymore, you no-place-like-home, self-deluded mother fucker." He stood a head taller than John, and he was so close that his broad shoulders created an eclipse against the overhead fluorescent lights.

"Don't touch me," John said and batted Rupert's hand away.

"Kids," Suga said. "Chill."

They kept walking and calling. Then, the hallway finally widened into a large room swarming with people in black t-shirts and headphones.

"He's here," one of them said, looking at John and Suga. John looked behind, saw no one, and then he looked back at the guy in the headphones again. It was only then that John realized that he himself was the center of their attention. Then the swarm seemed instantly to part and all activity stopped.

"What's going on?" John said, continuing to walk toward the commotion. The guys in black t-shirts said nothing back as he reached them, studied their faces.

Ahead Ian appeared, standing there smiling at him. "Hello, Sweetie," he said. "So glad you could make it."

"Make what?"

"Dog....," Suga was saying. "Dog, stop. Turn around and look at me."

Then Ian gestured in a grand, sweeping motion toward the stage, just ten feet or so further beyond. There, John could see Vivian and Stevie in the spotlight with someone else. John squinted. If his eyes could be believed, it was a minister in his full black collared outfit; he held a bible in one hand and Stevie's leash in the other. The crowd, just out of sight, clapped and whistled with impatience. The dog's back was hunched and his tail was between his legs. Stevie's eyes were open so wide, John could see the whites, even from where he stood.

He didn't take the time to think about what the hell was going on. "Dog," Suga was saying, but John could hardly hear him. John strode straight past the rest of the black t-shirt people with their clipboards and past the smirking Ian and right onto the stage. Between the roar of the crowd and the white baking heat from the lights, it was like, if he'd closed his eyes, he would think he was on a South Pacific beach with wild thundering surf, the kind that could kill you. He barely took note of the crowd howling for him in tribute. Up close, Vivian looked sweaty and lost, like maybe she would faint or start humming the theme tune to "Dallas," something she often did when she was drifting off to sleep.

Stevie was whimpering and straining toward John. "Hold on—" John said, grabbing the dog's leash from the minister's hand. "What the fuck are you doing?" he whispered to Vivian through his teeth. "Are you really this desperate?" He wanted to punch her and the feeling scared him.

Vivian came closer, covering the microphone attached to her white halter top. "This will be the making of us both," she said. "Posh and Becks. Jordan and Peter." John could almost hear Ian's voice as she spoke.

"Look, this is not going to happen. I'm going to sack Ian tomorrow anyway."

Vivian's eyes brightened and her jaw set tight. She looked for the first time all day like the normal version of herself. "This is live television, you self-centered cunt," she said to John. "After the way I've carried you—" Then she shrieked and looked down. "What the—" Stevie had his leg cocked and was urinating on her white skirt.

Vivian reared back and then slapped John, hard. It must have taken only a second, but he could see her hand coming for ages. She slapped him so hard there wasn't any pain at first, but he could feel the precise outlines of each finger and even her thumb.

The dog was shaking such that he lost his balance mid-stream and had to skitter back to his feet. He then proceeded to lose his marbles entirely. The slap was like the gesture a hypnotist might use to bring a person back into the room, only it seemed to have had the opposite effect on Stevie, sending him elsewhere, someplace dark and terrifying. His lips retracted and he barked at Vivian, a quick succession of deep sharp rips, his teeth bared and glistening with saliva. He had the body language of a junkyard Doberman. She flinched, leapt back, but the movement only agitated him further. The dog snarled and launched himself at Vivian's chest with real force, knocking her to the ground, snapping at her face.

Pop Idol security staff rushed onto the stage toward Stevie. John didn't have time to think how to react. With more grace and speed than John could have imagined, Rupert swooped past him. He picked up the dog in two hands like nothing more than a stuffed animal, like no more weight than sackcloth and sawdust, and he thrust the terrified creature toward John. John stumbled back and ran into Suga, who he hadn't even realized had followed him onto the stage.

Now, large men in yellow security jackets scuffled with Rupert. John and Suga were swept off in one direction and Vivian the other. John looked at her over his shoulder and saw her laughing, her mouth wide open, like a kid on a log flume.

He couldn't tell how many security guards' hands held him as they pushed him along, his feet hardly on the floor; he could see nothing but yellow and he lost sight of Suga. Even through the plastic jackets, the men's bodies reeked of stale beer, curry, drugstore cologne. One hand gripped the back of John's neck, pushing him forward even when there was no place to go, even when his face pressed into the back of the man in front of him and he could smell the musty chemical scent of the plastic.

He clutched Stevie to him, as if the animal were a thick pole he could grasp, something to steady him against the violent torrent, but the dog was writhing, the muscles of his torso flexing against all of the strength in John's arms. The dog jerked one way, and then back at John, its hard skull hammering his face. John felt blood flowing freely from his own nose, but still he held his grip on Stevie. The dog's heart raced under his fingers, like a bird battering itself into a window.

"Stevie. Stevie," he pleaded. "Calm down, boy." Foamy saliva dripped onto his hands, and then the dog went rigid and still, his legs pointed like a dancer's.

The large men shoving them along deposited John in a corner jumbled with amps and mixing equipment just off stage. "Get control of that dog," one of the guards said. The man's teeth overlapped chaotically in his mouth, like he had double the number he needed, and it made him look like he had fangs himself. With that, they all backed away a few steps.

John heard a loud wheezing sound, and Stevie's body began to shake in a way he had only seen on medical dramas. He sat on the floor and gathered Stevie to him, held his body and all of its violent contractions to his chest. The convulsions dissipated a little, but the dog's eyes were vacant and his mouth hung open. John wondered then if the dog was having a heart attack, if he had literally been scared to death. "Stevie, come on, boy." He sniffed, and wiped his palm across his lip, smearing the blood. He searched for any hint of recognition in Stevie's face, for a weak thump of his black tail.

Then, John did the only thing he could do. He put his mouth in the dog's ear, made his lips into an "o," and, quietly at first, but then louder and louder, he called forth a sound from deep in his gut. The sound travelled from John's body over the heads of the people on the stage. It went into the microphones. It filled the auditorium, silencing the raucous crowd in the darkness. It snaked between Ian and Vivian, skimming the surface of the glare they gave one another. It went through Rupert's legs, travelled the length of his body, and massaged the hands of the men who held him, loosening their grips. It vibrated through Suga's fingertips, which rested on John's shoulders, and raced up his arms and neck, encircling Suga's forehead like the headdress of a warrior.

It was not the thin "woo woooo" of celebration, as it had once been. It was instead now the low wail of the wolf, a complex cry from one battered, lonely creature to another that said, "I am here, but where is that?"

80

The Dispossession of Billy Montgomery

Billy Montgomery, thirty-nine years old and at his wits end, was squatting on top of the toilet lid in the stall at The El Corazon Disco Lounge. It was a cramped space, but he needed to be alone, where no one could see him. He held the gun in his shaking hands, the gun he had bought that afternoon at a pawnshop just outside the Smoky Ordinary town limits. Who knew that would be so easy to do? It was a miracle despondent teenagers hadn't bought out the entire stock. The fluorescent lights were flickering, casting strange, intermittent shadows on the bathroom ceiling. Graffiti on the stall wall asserted that Mo-Mo sucked his own cock, to which someone else had remarked, "Mo-Mo's a lucky limber bastard."

The rhythm of Billy's heart throbbed in his fingertips. Sweat trickled down his breastbone. He turned the gun until he could see down into its barrel. He studied the dark nothingness, thought, You can do this, you piece of chicken shit. Don't think. Just do it. The gun had heft, a solid weight in his hands, like it belonged there. Like it knew its duty, and could fulfill it. He wasn't afraid to die.

He was, however, afraid of pulling the trigger: for one, the violence of it—the noise, the blood, the mess. And more frightening, the possibility that someone might save him, and that he might become a vegetable or a cripple. He didn't like to picture his wife, Margeaux, and Sunny, his other wife, his non-legal wife, taking turns wiping his ass.

He wanted to remove himself from their lives cleanly. He wanted, for once in his life, to be selfless like his late father, the Reverend Bill Senior. Ironically enough, Billy had turned out to be just the sort of man that his father would have tried to rescue. But as Billy had often told his father, passing judgment on all those wretched souls, he didn't deserve rescuing. After the mess he'd made, he deserved to have his ticket punched. Billy adjusted the gun. Right here. Right in the cornea. Just concentrate.

And then, two guys came in to take a piss. Billy froze, tried to control his breathing. He listened to them walk over to the urinals and unzip, and to the echo of piss hitting porcelain. Billy tried again to concentrate on the death that was waiting for him, the relief of it. Careful not to knock the gun against the stall wall, he wiped the sweat from his forehead with his sleeve, tried to keep centered on himself. It was fine that they were there. People used bathrooms in disco lounges. They had the right.

As they were zipping up, the two guys began talking. Billy worked to ignore them, managed to concentrate on his breathing, to tune them out for the most part, but then one guy made a passing remark, something intended to be complimentary, about the other guy's sister. Something about her luscious onion of an ass.

Billy rolled his eyes and mouthed the word Jesus to himself. The one thing a guy should never do is open his mouth about another guy's sister. Even Billy, complete fuck-up that he was when it came to women, knew that. Because, he thought, the only thing worse than insinuating you wanted to screw a guy's sister was, when you got called on it, declaring that you didn't, that the sister wasn't at all attractive. You really couldn't win. And that was one thing Billy was an expert on—no-win situations.

And then, also, it was a particularly bad idea to talk shit about someone's sister in this place, the El Corazon. It wasn't a gentle place, not like the martini bars he went to with the guys from work, not the kind of place that soft-skinned, suit-wearing guys from Atkinson Publishing would like. It was a place where men in fatigues sat at tables by themselves all day and where the tattooed kids from the housing project always tried to get served underage, mostly with success. There were Christmas lights up year round, dusty and dim, and scores of stuffed and mounted dead animals on the walls, some of them wearing hats or lingerie, some of them decaying, the false noses and eyes exposed. It was one of the places that Billy's band, The Lonesome Rangers, played a lot, which was why he had decided to die here. It was the closest thing he had to a comfortable space.

It had been hard to find somewhere to die. One of the problems with being dispossessed, Billy had realized, was that there was no space that was just yours, where you had the privacy to jerk off or eat pork rinds off your chest or shoot yourself. He supposed he could have shot himself out in the woods, but crows might pick at his flesh and stray dogs might drag his body back into town. That would be humiliating. Alternatively, he could have offed himself at his mother's house, where he had been staying since he'd finally done the right thing and left Sunny. He'd left her after she said that she was having his baby. It was another one of her lies, another ploy to hold onto him, to keep him from trying to get back into Margeaux's good graces. But he had suddenly realized that Sunny's lie, the fake baby, was no worse than his own. After all, he had fake married her, had gone through the sham of a ceremony but had never filed the papers with the state of Virginia—because he was of course already married to Margeaux. He and Sunny could have kept trying to outdo each other until they both went into fake comas or something, but somewhere there had to be a limit. Somehow, he had to stop the cycle. Anyway, it seemed to him that on top of so much bad behavior, shooting himself at his widowed mother's house would have been too unkind, too ungrateful.

So he was here in the El Corazon Disco Lounge, and now two guys were in a heap on the bathroom floor, discovering the truth about bad-mouthing sisters, rabbit punching each other and grunting and swearing. Billy sighed and put his head in his hands, resting his forehead on top of the gun, waiting for them to finish and get out. He could wait. They were a temporary obstacle to his work.

After another minute, he heard the squeak of the door opening again. Whoever it was obviously couldn't get in, not with the two idiots wrestling on the floor, and so he just stood there with the door open. From the hallway, a breeze of malt liquor and cigarette smoke and jalapeno peppers came in, and carried on that breeze was the faintest sound of Veronica Hawksworth's voice.

Even though she sang for The Lonesome Rangers, his own band, it was suddenly as if Billy had never heard her before, or maybe had never listened. Her voice, Billy thought, sounded like honey and sandpaper, so deep but also unmistakably feminine. She was singing "Angel from Montgomery" on the karaoke machine, a song she often did when they played together. "That's my song," he would joke, after she finished and the applause died down. "You owe me a dollar." She got to expecting the line, and at one show reached down her shirt and pulled out a twenty, to hoots from the audience. How could he have forgotten about Veronica Hawksworth's voice—that there were things so beautiful in the world? He smiled, his forehead still resting on the gun, and he closed his eyes and he traced the shapes of the notes in his mind. He imagined for a moment that this was all there was—just him and that voice. He could see himself floating in a wonderful white emptiness, intertwined with nothing but the sound. Here, he would never see the terrible haunting sadness of women's eyes—Margeaux's, Sunny's, his mother's. This was how his life could have felt, if he had been someone else, someone brave enough to end it with Sunny, or smart enough never to have started it, and certainly never to have started those lesser things he'd had with other girls—Amber from Accounts, Molly the waitress, that police woman from Garstang.

Now, in this lovely empty space with the music, Billy could picture Margeaux's face as it was before all of this started, her creamy skin and dark hair, her faintly hooked nose, the dimples that appeared whenever she tried not to laugh. Those intelligent dark eyes, the way there seemed to be thoughts swirling behind them always just beyond his reach. Listening to Veronica Hawksworth's voice, he imagined his life with Margeaux as it should have been, as it was meant to be. Simple and beautiful, a sustained, full-bodied note. Veronica's voice was magic, and he felt in love with Margeaux again.

One of the guys wrestling on the floor started screaming. "Oh God," he yelled, "my eye!"

Billy stood up slowly, his legs cramped and tingling, and he peered over the top of the stall. He saw the man who was holding the door open, little and bald, just sort of standing there like he was waiting for a bus or something. Over by the urinals were the two wrestling guys, one of them with a hand over his face and feeling around on the floor, sputtering a steady stream of obscenities. He was skinny and he wore lace-up boots under his jeans and a pink WMAX T-shirt.

"Hey," Billy said calmly. "Can you guys shut up? I'm trying to hear the music."

Pink T-shirt continued crawling around. "If I've lost my eye," he said to the other guy, "you're going to fucking pay for it."

"The fuck I am," said the other guy, who was lying on his back, panting. Blood trickled from the side of his mouth into his scraggly goatee. He was a little chunky. "That fucking eye is creepy as hell. Be glad it's gone."

"You take that back!" Pink T-shirt said, turning around. "That is a fucking top-quality eye. It came all the way from fucking France, you big ass."

"The only big ass in this place is your fucking sister's," the other guy muttered.

Pink T-shirt turned. He took his hand away from the shriveled eye socket. "You stop thinking about my sister's ass," he growled. He got to his feet, and with surprising speed, kicked Goatee Guy in the face before he had time to flinch away. Blood splattered the floor. Goatee Guy began to scream in a way that Billy had dreamed of for the last month. His nose was smeared across his cheek, as if it had been made of clay, and he clutched his face with one hand and reached for Pink T-shirt's leg with the other. He yanked up Pink T-shirt's pant leg and bit him on the calf, just above the boot. Pink T-shirt bellowed, trying to shake his leg loose and reaching for a heavy wooden toilet plunger that sat in the corner of the bathroom.

Heat rose from the center of Billy's chest, up into his throat. He pinched his eyes closed and he slammed the gun against the stall several times. "Shut up," he yelled. "I will fucking shoot you both if I don't get to hear the end of this song."

Pink T-shirt froze, the toilet plunger raised over his head, and he stared at Billy as if he were seeing him for the first time, one brown eye wide and nervous, the other little more than a flap, a deep black void, like the barrel of the gun.

"Whoa," Goatee Guy said, his head back on the floor, his hands in the air. "Relax."

"I will not relax," said Billy, pointing the gun at him. "Until you shut up."

"Okay, dude," Pink T-shirt said. He lowered the toilet plunger and gingerly set it down. He put his hands up as well. Blood trickled down his boot. "Shutting up's no problem."

"Yeah," said the other guy. "We love music."

"Do you know us, dude? I'm Paul," Pink T-shirt said, pointing to himself. "And that's Ernest, a.k.a. Wild Man. Paul and Wild Man in the Morning? WMAX?"

"We can get you free CD's," said the guy on the floor hopefully. Blood covered his face, staining his teeth too. His voice was low-pitched and nasal now, like he had a cold.

Billy closed his eyes. "Shut up," he whispered.

"Sure, okay," Paul whispered back, and then he lowered himself next to his friend.

Standing on top of the toilet, the gun's barrel resting on the top of the stall door, pointing at the radio brawlers, Billy tried to concentrate again, this new silence like water in a boat's wake, rippling. He breathed deeply and exhaled, relaxed his shoulders. He tried to find Veronica's voice, tried to find that whiteness, that floating feeling. He leaned into the quiet and began to make out the words again.

And then the door squeaked shut. Billy opened his eyes. Paul and Wild Man were still staring at him, their hands quivering above their heads, but the little bald guy was gone and so was the breeze from the hallway and so was the music. With a groan, Billy turned the gun and pointed it at his own head.

"Whoa, hey," said Wild Man, sitting up, flinching with obvious pain. "What are you doing?"

"What does it look like?"

"If this is about a woman that don't love you no more," Paul said, "she's not worth it, whoever she is."

Billy thought of Margeaux, how he'd humiliated her, how she deserved so much better, and he smiled weakly. "That's just not true," he said.

"No, this is my territory," Paul said. "Do you know how many guys have offed themselves because of my sister?"

"I know," said Wild Man, bringing his hand to his goatee and then looking up. "Two. Is it two?"

"That's right, moron. Two," said Paul. "And both of them shouldn't have done it." He turned to Billy then. "Why do you think I'm trying to keep this genius away from her?"

Wild Man turned to Paul with surprise. "Hey, that's sweet," he said. "Are you, really?"

"What are friends for?"

"Shut up," Billy said. "It's not the same thing. I know what I'm doing." He nodded toward the door, and then he cocked the hammer. "You guys can leave if you want."

"No. Wait, just wait," Paul said in a drawn-out way. "What if we played your band on the radio or something. Chicks love musicians. Maybe you can get her back. Or maybe you can get another girl, a really good one."

Billy tilted his head and lowered the gun. "How do you know about my band?"

"What, are you kidding?" said Wild Man, still sitting on the floor. He laughed nervously. "We come here all the time. You guys are awesome."

"Do you really think so?" Billy said. He smiled sadly. He thought about Veronica's voice. If there was one thing in his life worth sticking around for, maybe that was it. He thought about Margeaux again, her face as it had been in his daydream with the music, contented and peaceful, without the burden of his mistakes. Maybe somehow the music, the music he and Veronica played, could take him back to that place for real, a place where Margeaux's eyes weren't pained and hollow. Maybe it would help him find a way. Not that he expected her to love him again. If she just didn't hate him. That would be something.

"We've been talking about it, haven't we, Ernie?" Paul said to Wild Man, who nodded enthusiastically, blood bubbling at one nostril. "Yuck, man," Paul said. "Tip your head back, like this," he suggested, pinching the bridge of his own nose.

"Yeah, we want to have a local showcase on the program," Wild Man said, addressing the ceiling in a pinched-nose nasal twang. "Maybe have you guys, County Seat, Dale & Erv, The Lunch Ladies, people like that. What do you think?"

"Really," said Paul, "I need you to do this. Listen, I didn't do so good with those other guys who offed themselves for my sister. One of them was a good pal. So, be a sport, will you?"

The bathroom door squeaked open a crack, then, and they all turned to see who it was.

Billy saw first the signature pink handkerchief, worn as a head scarf thing, sort of like a bathing cap. It was Veronica, and the color of her round face was uneven under the fluorescent lights. It made him think of the moon, or a wheel of cheese, or something. And yet she was beautiful, those enormous brown eyes that had somehow retained an innocence in spite of everything—working in a factory for seven years, scraping her way up to dental receptionist, taking care of her sick parents, dealing with the death of her repairman husband, who at the age of forty-five fell from the town water tower and was impaled on a piece of rebar sticking out of an unfinished concrete block wall. "Billy? What's going on?" She surveyed the room. "For Pete's sake, what are you trying to do, kill yourself?"

It rattled Billy to have her say it. It was as if he really mattered to her. And if that was true. . . . He stuffed the gun down the back of his pants. "Well—"

"Because leaning your head back like that is dangerous," she said. She was talking to Wild Man. "You'll choke on your own blood."

Billy slumped against the stall wall and shook his head in resignation. It just wasn't going to happen. This was a dispossession that took away everything, not just his home and TV and privacy and two wives, real and fake, but even the right to put an end to it all.

He smiled—much too broadly, really, to be believable, even by himself. He sniffed, wiped his nose, and cleared his throat, as if it were true that nothing was really happening, as if it was the most normal thing in the world to be standing on the toilet, talking over the stall door to two guys who had done such a number on each other that they looked like extras from Carrie. "Hey, guess what," he said to Veronica. "Guess who they are." He pointed to Paul and Wild Man, who were smoothing their hair and their clothes, smiling as if it were school picture day. Exactly how it would look if the El Corazon had picture day.

Veronica paused, squinting at Billy for a moment, pulling her chin back quizzically. She opened her mouth, her pale lips quivering. "Well, I don't know."

Billy jumped down from the toilet and burst from the stall. "Hey, don't worry. I have great news," he said, going to her with open arms. He looked over his shoulder. "Isn't that right, guys?"

"That's right," Paul said. His single eye flitted to Billy's waist, where the gun stuck out.

"Hey," said Billy, lunging toward the floor. "I found your eye!" He scooped it up, slick and cold, and gave it to Wild Man, who gave it to Paul, palm open and the eye in the center like a peace offering.

"There, you see?" said Billy. "It's a sign." He watched Paul hold the eye up to the light, inspecting it, and he couldn't help feeling it was watching him, but not the way he often felt like his father watched him, from somewhere far up in the sky above. No, the eye watched him from somewhere closer—from a vantage point where it could see Billy's mistakes exactly as they were, not distorted by the distance. They weren't, to be fair to himself, crimes of short-sightedness, but rather of expansiveness, for example, a sort of double-jointed ability to love more than one person at once. And what was wrong with that, really?

Billy reached over and gave Veronica a squeeze. "I heard you sing, you know. But there's no charge this time. By the way, do you have any idea how wonderful you are?" he said.

She smiled and wiped at the sweat on her upper lip, the way a woman does when she feels singled out, on top of the world.

Missing Person

Dori's husband, Hank, who was dying of a brain tumor, had been in Dr. Feiffer's office at Fauquier County General for over an hour, long enough for Dori to get irritated by the group of nurses in the hallway, who were laughing about a television program they'd all seen. It was a report about a man who had such a terrible gas problem he couldn't leave the house. Dori hadn't been able to stomach television news for weeks.

"I think it's noble," one of them piped up. "He shuts himself away out of respect for other people."

"He's not noble," said another nurse. "He's embarrassed. As he should be." This led to a discussion of their own deep dark social problems, such as wayward hair and mysterious rashes. So much of life, Dori thought, was a struggle against unseemliness. She scooted down from her brother, Lewis, and looked out the window at the flowers and budding trees, which seemed stunned by the late cold snap that had hit Northern Virginia—including Brilliant, where the hospital was, as well as her own town, Smoky Ordinary, just down the road. She closed her eyes and tried to call up the words to a song from *My Fair Lady*, a play she had seen a dozen times, to help her ignore the nurses.

Up until three months earlier, when Hank got sick, Dori had been a waitress at The Lazy Susan Dinner Theater, the third-largest dinner theater in the DC area. So she had seen a lot of musicals, even though she was only twenty-five and not in her sixties like most of the customers. It occurred to her now that her own life would never be a musical; a Broadway-style song about cancer, even sung to a sad melody, would just be in bad taste. In the musicals performed at the Lazy Susan, people overcame their unseemly problems. And if someone died, the death was either noble, a sacrifice of great courage, or tragic, the consequence of one moment's passion or dooming foolishness. People never wasted away, their bodies ravaging themselves. Besides, what rhymed with chemotherapy? Pee no carrots please. Or radiation? Stay free nation!

She turned and glared at Lewis, who elbowed her arm every time he flipped a page of *Field and Stream*. He was only looking at the pictures, so he bumped into her at a rapid-fire pace. That was the model for their relationship right now: Lewis had come to live with her and Hank five months earlier, in November after he finished a three-year prison sentence for committing a robbery. He needed some help getting back on his feet, and now Dori was always stumbling over him. He seemed unable to do anything on his own.

"What?" he said, looking up.

Dori shook her head. She saw Dr. Feiffer coming down the hall, maybe with news about Hank's CAT Scan, and she grabbed Lewis's magazine and held it on her lap. Dr. Feiffer's coat flapped open with his athletic strides. He looked to be, what? Thirty-five? Younger than Hank. The age when people can still expect perfect health. She had become obsessed with people's ages lately.

"Listen, Mrs. Mallone," Dr. Feiffer said when he reached her. "Hank is gone—"

"Oh, God," Lewis interrupted and then he stood up, his right ankle buckling a little. A family across the room looked up from their magazines, their faces taking on the gray color of the wallpaper.

"No. It's not that," the doctor whispered.

Nothing, not the hand on his hip or the tight lines of his forehead, told Dori not to worry, the way she wanted. "Don't be stupid," Dori said to Lewis. "Let the doctor speak. Hank's fine. He's doing great." She forced a laugh. After all, he wasn't that old, only fifteen years older than she was, and that should count for something.

Dr. Feiffer looked past her for a moment toward the children's play area, with its red plastic furniture and its unconvincing picture books about heaven, and then he went on, as if Dori hadn't said anything. "A technician was prepping your husband in an exam room," he explained. "She was called away for just a moment, and when she returned, he was gone. He wasn't in the hall or in the restroom or in any of the rooms nearby." He went on to say that earlier, before Hank slipped out of the room, he had been thanking the hospital staff, clasping their hands, patting their backs.

"Oh no," Lewis said.

"Hank's losing it, and you just leave him alone?" Dori said. "What's going on with you people?"

"He appeared quite lucid, and he was acting very friendly, which is often disarming to staff," Dr. Feiffer said. "He may have thought he was cured. That happens sometimes." He looked from Dori to Lewis, and back to her. "People are looking already, but we may need you to help us talk to him when we find him," he said quietly.

Dori peered into Dr. Feiffer's brown eyes and imagined how they might soften later as he ate dinner with his family, and for a moment envy replaced fear, and she wished she could step into that world, as Dr. Feiffer's wife, or even as his daughter.

To not have to tell Hank, when he'd forget every few days, that the reason he didn't feel well was that he had terminal cancer. . . . She wouldn't have to see him tear up in his quiet, resigned way, like part of him remembered all along, and she wouldn't have to hear him call to his dog Sonny, who had been dead for four years—since before Dori and Hank had met during Lewis's trial and started going out for coffee together. Dr. Feiffer had told her to be direct with Hank, to say, "You have brain cancer. It's terminal. But we're here for you." She had given Hank this speech twenty times, and now it seemed like it had backfired. He'd gone from not remembering he was sick to believing he was cured. Dori wondered if Dr. Feiffer would make her give Hank a new speech after they found him, something equally difficult like, "You're not cured. And you probably won't live much longer. Now give me a hug."

But Dr. Feiffer didn't do that yet. Instead, he described where the orderlies were already combing the building for Hank and drew her a map of the hospital on a pad that said "From the desk of Dr. Terry Feiffer." He said he would keep her posted, and would tell them immediately when Hank was found.

After he left, Dori and Lewis split up to check the halls and stairwells themselves. She watched Lewis jog around the corner, toward intensive care. And then she searched for quite a while on her own, but it seemed that all she saw under the weak fluorescent lights was a blur of pasty-faced patients in their rooms, people who turned toward her with mild interest as she passed, the way cows did along the highway. Could she check every empty bed, every closet-sized bathroom? Empty gurneys lurked along the corridors and seemed dangerous, like they were calculating who would need them next. In the maternity ward, where a mother shuffled down the hallway in new slippers, Dori thought again about a time before Hank got sick, when she told him she felt too young for a baby. She remembered his disappointed but accepting reaction, his always gentle face, like warm bread.

What she hadn't told him was that she didn't want to feel permanently tied to him. As she turned the corner and passed the nursery, she told
herself that she wouldn't have time to take care of a baby now anyway.
Her sneakers tapped a rhythm on the metal lip of concrete steps and on
speckled floors and gradually, they began to wear raw spots on her bare
ankles, wounds she regarded indifferently, nuisances she didn't have the
time or energy to acknowledge. When Dori finally met up again with
her brother on the sixth floor, he looked at his watch. "It's been half an
hour," he said. "What if Hank got outside?"

Dori went to the nurse's station then to see if anyone had called the
police, and Lewis went to the end of the hallway, waited, and rapped on
the elevator doors, as if this might make them open sooner. He yelled
that he would be outside checking the grounds.

When Dori stepped into the unseasonably cool April afternoon to find
Lewis, no one at all was visible: the shrubs and clipped grass wore on
as far as she could see; even the bloated clouds retreated, making the
world impossibly huge. She looked out at the series of parking lots
and finally saw Lewis perched on a yellow curbstone, peering over the
rows and rows of cars hunched together under the gray sky. His slight
frame curved at the shoulders just like when he was a kid, only then it
made him look sensitive, maybe bookish, and now it always made him
look like he was plotting something, and already feeling guilty. Only
the faintest bit of blond stubble mottled his chin, even though he hadn't
shaven in probably a week. Maybe because he had been in prison, Dori
often forgot he was just twenty-two, three years younger than she was.
Now, his cowlick poking up at the back of his head, his sneakers flashy
like a sports star's as he jumped to see over the cars, it was as if he was
twelve again, as if he were the equally unreliable counterpart of her fail-
ing husband.

Still, hidden in Lewis's boyish body was a wiry strength that allowed
him to restrain Hank when he tried to hit the people he saw on the television, and to pull him up the stairs every night for bed, even though Hank
was taller and weighed more. Picturing Lewis with Hank's limp body
on his back, Dori thought about the arbitrariness of the whole situation.
If Hank, who was a bailiff, hadn't been assigned to work with that judge
on that day, she would never have met him, and none of this would involve her. She would be a twenty-five-year-old waitress—nothing more
complicated. In a way, all of this was Lewis's fault for holding up that
mini-mart in the first place.

"We're never going to find him," Lewis said, stuffing his hands into the pockets of his uniform. He was supposed to go to his job at the Brilliant Holiday Inn—where he was a security guard, of all things—after Hank's appointment at the hospital. He had gotten the job because Hank had pulled some strings with a friend back in November, when Lewis finished his three years and came to live with them.

"Don't talk that way," Dori said. "We don't have a choice. You better call and tell them you're not coming in today."

"I can call from the car," he said, and when Dori stared, puzzled, he sighed and flung his hands in the air. "We have to drive around and look for him. That's what you do when people are lost."

Dori supposed it was a good idea, though she didn't want to say so. Lewis's common sense irritated her, maybe because she thought he often pretended that he didn't have any. But it was true that if Hank was still inside, someone would probably find him; if he had made it outside, anything could happen. The police had said no officers could get to Hank's case for at least an hour because they were busy tending to a gas tanker that was overturned on the interstate. The whole thing was closed in both directions and people had been trapped there since morning rush hour.

The cheese sandwich Dori had eaten earlier, in the hospital cafeteria, rose to her throat when she thought about Hank confused, lost, wondering where he was. When Hank was first diagnosed, Dr. Feiffer had explained that the tumor was spider-shaped, which was why they couldn't remove all of it. It had legs in parts of Hank's brain that the surgeons couldn't touch. Dori pictured those spider legs moving Hank along now instead of his own legs. Where would they take him? She closed her eyes.

"Dori?" Lewis said. "Hello?" When she opened her eyes, Lewis looked like he might slap her, the way men in disaster movies were always slapping people who'd fainted.

"Let's go," she said curtly.

Dori normally rode in the back with Hank to make sure he kept his hands away from the door latch. Sitting in the passenger seat reminded her of a good day last month, when she'd let Hank drive the car around the block. "I miss driving," he had said, and revved the engine. "How about I open her up? See what's under the hood?"

"Whoa! Whoa!" Dori had said, her arms flailing.

"Just kidding," he said, looking a little hurt. "But I gotcha, though, didn't I?" He had wanted to have sex that night, but it was too physically demanding and he fell asleep. Dori had felt so relieved; she got up and cleaned the bathroom.

After Lewis called the Holiday Inn, he slowly pulled out of the parking lot and Dori squinted, trying to see the million hidden places Hank could be—in a thick grove of trees beyond the bus stop, in the back seat of an unlocked car, or maybe between the off-duty ambulances, which were fenced in and looked somber, like old horses. Hank had wandered before, but always out the back door of their house to the creek in the woods, like he was trying to remember the plan he'd had to divert the water and make a small fish pond in their yard.

This time felt different, though, and Dori let herself think about what it would be like if he stayed gone. She remembered the life she had before they were married—taking courses at the community college, spending evenings and weekends waitressing or talking with her girlfriends, reading novels in the garage apartment she used to rent. For a moment, she thought maybe she could just drive away from the hospital and get her old life back. She could try out for the plays at the dinner theater, instead of standing timidly in the back, mouthing all the lines. But then she thought about where Hank might be and the many ways people wouldn't understand him, might even be cruel. Maybe someone had already yelled at him for standing in the middle of the road or for touching a stranger's arm. Maybe Hank had already approached a salesclerk or cashier and said, "Late for Ed," his eyes and nose twitching with agitation. And whoever he was talking to didn't know how to calm him down because they didn't know that Ed was Hank's old boss and that every morning Hank thought he had a meeting to go to. They didn't know to say, "The meeting is cancelled," and to give him a bagel with cream cheese, which was his favorite.

Dori and Lewis scanned the sidewalks scattered with rainbow-slicked puddles. Some gas station attendants sat in folding chairs in front of the Exxon, not speaking, their faces worn as tree knots. Dori looked for knowledge of Hank. Maybe just the shuffle of a black boot could mean they'd seen him—his graying brown hair, his sloping shoulders, his green and black shirt, his Levi's. He had always dressed stylishly and Dori had tried to keep him the way he used to be, if for no other reason than the slight smile when he saw himself in the mirror.

Lewis took his hand from the steering wheel and tousled his own hair. "What if we don't find him?" he said, and switched on the radio's music of garbled talk; then he clicked it off again. "I'll tell you, I might flip out and do something stupid."

"Get real," said Dori. "You're not as delicate as you like to pretend." She glared at him, but really she didn't know if what she said was true or not. When Lewis first came to stay with them, he hung on Hank's every word, especially when Hank talked about political matters, saying things like "Who looks out for the common man anymore? It's all special interests and big money." Lewis brought lunch to Hank at work several days a week. He even offered to do Hank's chores, like raking the grass and doing the dishes—things Lewis had never done when he and Dori lived at home, in the trailer park with their mother.

One night when Lewis was up to his elbows in sudsy water, Dori asked him why he robbed that mini-mart in the first place, and he said, "I don't know. I guess I wanted some smokes and a long vacation." Dori thought how Lewis liked to act as though everything that ever happened was fine, maybe even for the best. But she knew he didn't believe it. He only wanted to. That way, he could be irresponsible and not feel bad about it.

Since Hank had gotten sick, Lewis had started doing even more chores, like laundry and cooking. But he'd also started smoking again and getting phone calls from the people he knew before prison. Lately, he spent long hours on the front porch, staring out at the traffic or drawing on the back of his hand in magic marker. He almost never called his girlfriend, Sharla, who was the manager of the Hallmark store in downtown Smoky Ordinary and who had been open-minded about him when a lot of his other high school friends weren't. Dori felt so sorry for Sharla when Lewis wouldn't take her calls that she had started making small talk and now the two of them were becoming good friends. Last night, Dori thought, Sharla had planned to tell Lewis about her pregnancy.

Sharla had said she didn't know whether she should even mention it to Dori, which hurt to hear, although it made sense. Even though Dori tried to remember other people's problems, it was hard. She thought how for some people, this self-centeredness was a normal state of mind. Until lately, she'd always considered Lewis one of those people. She looked at his profile, his straight freckled nose. If Sharla had told him, he hadn't said.

"I never said I was delicate," Lewis said to Dori. "Think about it. Delicate people don't do too well in penitentiaries." He turned the car down Boxwood Street, past the McDonalds and the First Virginia Bank and the maple trees just sprouting late buds. Brilliant was enormous compared to Smoky Ordinary; the area surrounding the hospital was a geometrical maze of strip malls and pale yellow housing developments and massive highways with no sidewalks next to them.

"Well, what are you saying then?" Dori said.

"That I actually.... Oh, nothing. Forget it," he said. "You wouldn't understand."

"I wouldn't?" Dori said. "Don't you think I have feelings? You're not the center of the universe." She opened the glove compartment and plucked out a tissue. She almost never cried, because when she did, Hank cried, too, and it was hard to get him to stop. "Slow down," she said then, because she saw a crowd of people in front of a coffee shop. She craned out the window and asked a young woman wearing a brown ball cap if she'd seen anyone who looked like Hank; the woman said no. "I guess not," Dori said to Lewis. "Keep going."

Lewis pulled back into traffic, looking over his shoulder, the same expression on his face as when he used to concentrate on something like collecting skipping stones from the gravel road that ran through the trailer park south of Smoky Ordinary, where their mother still lived. Now it was the expression he gave to show that his feelings were hurt.

She thought about the nest of magazine and newspaper clippings she'd found in Lewis's room just a few days earlier, consumer reports about the best car stereos, radar detectors, and other vehicle electronics, plus clipped-out ads for pawn shops, some all the way into the District and around the Beltway in Prince George's County. When she asked him about it, he became sullen and silent and finally left the house, coming back three hours later, in time to start Hank's dinner. Lewis offered to make pizza, Dori's favorite, and Dori ironed Lewis's uniform, maybe because, she thought now, those three hours apart gave them each a taste of being alone. Dori felt the crying inch away from her like an impacted sneeze.

"Let's call Mom," Lewis said. "And have her wait at the house in case Hank goes home."

"That's stupid. He won't make it that far," Dori told him. But she could think of no reason not to call except that she didn't want to involve her mother. Dori's mother had had a series of husbands when she and Lewis were growing up, several of whom had been rough with their mother in front of them. But the final husband, Macon Riggs, tried it one too many times. Dori's mother knocked him unconscious with a large bottle of olive oil and filed for divorce before he got the bandage off his head. "Men are a losing proposition," her mother said later.

"It's like I finally woke up and saw I wasn't getting anything back." Lewis—who had sometimes, late at night, promised that he would kill Macon Riggs—had been in the room for that conversation, and occasionally Dori wondered if he had taken their mother's words to include him. In his off-kilter way, he still seemed like he was trying to prove himself to her. As far as Dori could tell, her mother adored Lewis. Dori dialed her number.

When she answered the phone, Dori explained what had happened. "Well, what about you?" her mother said. "Are you okay? Is Lewis taking care of you?"

"I'm not the one who needs to be taken care of," Dori said.

Her mother cleared her throat and rattled some dishes into the sink. "I guess that depends on your perspective," she told Dori quietly. Dori's mother had gotten bolder in the six years since she left her last husband, and even more distrustful of men, Lewis excepted; she had recently suggested that Dori commit Hank to the Indian Summer Retirement Home, out on Rural Route 1. It happened because she had been in the living room one night last week while Dori gave Hank a shower in the downstairs bathroom, and he'd had his regular outburst.

"Damn it to hell, Rita," Hank had yelled. "Rita," the name of one of his old girlfriends, was all he ever called Dori anymore. Dori tried not to mind; she wanted to let the name make her feel like this was happening to someone else. But it embarrassed her, also; she guessed people like her mother wanted to know what it was about this Rita person that she stayed in his mind while Dori's name leaked out the way brown water leaked from weeks-old lettuce in her fridge.

"What's going on in there?" her mother said from the hallway.

"Nothing to worry about," Dori had yelled back. "It's all this medication. It makes him irritable." Thankfully, her mother couldn't see the way he punched the air near Dori's face or the way his cheek and eye twitched or the way his lean body had begun to shrink, his arms and legs scrawny and pale as an old man's, his torso melting loosely from his shoulders. Once, a year earlier, Dori and her mother had gone to Potomac Mills Mall, where they saw a man yelling at his wife at the jewelry counter at Nordstrom Rack. Dori's mother had told the man to screw himself and Dori had to hold her arms to keep her from trying to hit him. "Is this what you really want?" Dori's mother had said to the wife. "Why don't you think about yourself for a change?"

"Please don't say a word about nursing homes," Dori said to her now. "I know what you're thinking."

"Things could be different for you," her mother said.

"You and I aren't the same person. This is how things are for me," Dori told her, and to her own ear, she sounded assertive. She sounded like women in plays she'd seen at the Lazy Susan, people who rallied in a time of crisis. But Dori knew she wasn't really like that. She was more like the characters who got pulled into something, like a crime or an elaborate deceit, and then spent the rest of the play doing what they had to do to get through it.

"It's not worth it," her mother said.

"Mom," Dori said, feeling a flash of anger. "I know you've been with men who maybe don't deserve much, but Hank does. I married a good man. He's still a good man." Dori was glad to hear herself say that and she almost said it again because it felt so good to know those feelings were in there. She had the urge to say something positive about Lewis, too. But then she stopped. Even though Lewis's behavior as a teenager had been much worse than Dori's, their mother had seemed amused by it rather than alarmed. When Lewis stole money from their mother's purse, she called it his "allowance," as if he were entitled to it. He got enough undue praise.

"I know Hank's a good person," her mother said. "But he's hardly even there anymore."

"Enough," Dori said. "Can you just go over to the house and check for me?"

"Yes. Fine. I'll call you when I get there."

"What's with you two?" Lewis said after Dori hung up. Then he pointed to a man in a phone booth who had the same grayish brown hair as Hank, but the man's posture was too good. He looked too healthy.

Dori shook her head. "She was pressing about the nursing home again. She always knows how to say just the right thing." Dori watched a woman march a line of Brownies toward Ben and Jerry's on the corner of Boxwood and Smith, their knobby knees churning the air, the light flashing off their buttons and pins like a warning. A man's feet rested on the stoop in the Royale Drycleaner's entryway, but as Dori looked closer, she noticed his holey argyle socks, different from Hank's black ones with the gold toes, which she had wrestled onto his feet that morning. Side streets flickered past the window like dreams. If only they were in Smoky Ordinary, someone would recognize Hank. Someone would call.

Lewis fired up a cigarette with the glowing dashboard lighter and then scrutinized a line of men at a cash machine. "You can't do that,"

Lewis said and flicked his ash out the window. He looked at her then, his face tight. "You can't shut him away."

"I know," Dori said, hearing the disappointment in her own voice.

"I don't want to lose him," Lewis said. "I mean. . . ."

"I know," Dori said. And she actually did know what he meant. As long as they still had Hank, the situation wasn't okay exactly, but they could live with it. Increasingly incapacitated, he still bound them together. It was better than whatever was coming next. That's how it felt.

Dori rubbed away the mist that had formed on the glass beside her. As the car crept down a less populated block, she saw The American Grille, the last place she had taken Hank to lunch before he suddenly forgot the names of his co-workers and the words for "toothbrush" and "shirt" and they went to the doctor to see what was wrong. It was January, a gray day, and he was wearing the blue scarf she'd gotten him for Christmas. He laid it neatly over the back of his chair and ordered a club sandwich. Dori had revealed to him over crackers her fear that he might have an affair, what with their long hours apart, her working nights and him working overtime.

"Ridiculous," he had said, taking a sip of his tea. He'd had a cold for a few weeks, but neither of them thought much of it then. "I would never do that," he said, and Dori decided he was right. He never would; he was so firmly committed that he wasn't even bothered by her worry. The truth was that she was afraid that she might have an affair, though not with anyone in particular. It was just that when she was at the theater, the men her own age, waiters and bartenders who acted in the plays, were so excited and full of the future that Dori wanted to touch them. Hank seemed to have no questions about his life; it was as if it were a puzzle he'd already solved. Since then, she had always seen those feelings, that lunch, as a sign about how ill-suited the two of them were. But now, she wasn't so sure. At this moment, even if he were incoherent and angry, she would rather be holding his arm in the backseat than absorbing this sickening empty space. She had no idea what action to take, and it made her dizzy, like standing on top of the high dive during her last swimming lesson when she was seven, her mother treading water below, a desperate idea of the instructor's. "Jump, goddammit," her mother yelled. "You think I don't have better things to do?"

"We're almost back," Lewis said, referring to the large circle he'd made, which had brought them near the hospital again.

"I can see that," Dori said, too sharply, though she knew he only said it to be reassuring. He tapped his fingers on the dashboard like drumsticks, trying not to react. On the sidewalk, she saw a woman scolding a big brown dog as if it might see the error of its ways and make some life changes. There was so much pettiness, so much wasted time in life, she thought.

"Sometimes I think about taking things," Lewis said. "When I'm at work, I see a lot of unlocked cars. It would be pretty easy."

Dori looked over, ready to let loose on him. His hair rippled in the wind and he had his lips pressed tightly together, like he might accidentally say something else, what was really bothering him. It softened her, and she tried to think of some decent way to respond, but she was so tired. "Hank wouldn't want you to do that," she finally said. "He'd be disappointed."

"Yeah, I know," Lewis told her, and he kept drumming his fingers, tapping out some song she didn't know. "It's just that I want that stuff bad."

"Come on, Lewis."

"I do. I'm just telling the truth."

Dori ran a hand through her hair and then turned away, toward the window. "Well, what about Sharla?" she said. She kept her back to him then and didn't speak, but she listened to his breathing.

"What's the point? If this can happen to somebody like Hank, and to you. . . ." Lewis said and paused. He sounded like he might cry.

Dori turned toward him. "Lewis," she said, not because she didn't know what to say but because his name seemed important, like a secret they shared. She took his hand. "Don't leave me," she said.

He looked at her with surprise and then he caught himself and sniffled and wiped his nose with the back of his hand. And she realized then that he hadn't known this before—that anyone needed him.

My God, she thought. Did Hank know? Had he known that maybe she loved him more than she had wanted to let herself?

When they got to the hospital, they circled the grounds, skirting peonies and azalea bushes that hugged the monstrous white building, as if plants could pretty up what went on in there. A little girl picked up a tiny stone and whipped it at her sister while their grandfather waited by the entrance in a wheel chair. Dori strained to see into the corridor, imagining she'd see Hank slumped forward in one of the conjoined plastic chairs, or that she'd see Dr. Feiffer running toward them, grinning with good news about Hank's prognosis. But this was unlikely, impossible, and Dori understood that she was beginning to dislike Dr. Feiffer for all of the things he would say and not say.

The phone rang then, and when Dori answered, her mother told her that Hank wasn't at home. "Maybe I'll drive around the neighborhood," she said, "though I'm not sure it'll do any good. Then she paused and shuffled some papers, probably prescriptions and medical bills on the counter. "I'm not trying to be unkind, but I hope this doesn't go on much longer," she said.

Words scurried through Dori's head and then disappeared in dark corners. Her mother's ideas had been threatening when she was afraid they might sway her. But now she understood that she would never wish Hank dead, even though maybe she should, and her reasons weren't purely selfless, like her mother thought. What she wanted, she thought now, was simple: to be with Hank when he was scared, to listen to him when he talked gibberish, to feel him beside her for as many more nights as she could, their two bodies curled together like always. That part of his brain had not forgotten.

"Honey?" her mother said. "Are you there?"

"Yes, Momma," Dori said. Lewis pulled to a stop outside the emergency-room entrance.

"Your house is cold," her mother said. "I'm going to turn up the heat."

"We're trying to save some money," Dori said. "But it's fine if you do that," she added, and she thought for a moment how nice it would be to come home and find her mother snuggled into the couch cushions reading a mystery novel in her blue bathrobe, something she used to do a lot when Dori was a kid. It made her think about how hard it was to notice the things you liked while they were happening.

When she got off the phone, it rang again immediately. Lewis raised his eyebrows, and Dori rolled her eyes, and for a minute, the two of them smiled at each other. She answered the phone.

It was Dr. Feiffer. "I've got Hank here," he said.

"Oh, God," she said.

He explained that Hank had been found in a laundry room, a little shaken up, but okay. He was at the third floor nurses' station now, and they'd given him a Sprite and they were talking to him, which kept him calm, even though he didn't understand what they said. "I've rescheduled the CAT Scan. So, there's no harm done. I think he'll be okay to go home. We can try it again tomorrow."

After Dori hung up, she said to Lewis, "They found him."

But it was clear that Lewis already understood, and he turned down an aisle of cars to find a parking place. Dori waited to feel some relief, but it didn't come the way she felt like it would. Looking out at the things she'd hadn't seen lately—grass and dandelions and gray birds splashing in puddles—and then looking back at Lewis, she thought maybe that's what love was, something as hard to see as to ignore.

There wasn't a single person in the vast lot now, or on the icy smooth sidewalk, or under the brooding steel and glass awning that marked the entrance. Lewis pulled into a space and turned off the car. He let his head fall back and his arms go limp on the seat. "Do you think we'll remember this tomorrow?" Lewis said.

"Yeah," Dori laughed. "Lucky us."

Experiments

My father, appliance repairman Ed Hart, had been dating a reporter from the local news for over three months, ever since he and my mother separated. They met when Channel Four's "Eye on You" News interviewed me at the Northern Virginia Sixth Grade Science Fair about my winning project, The Worm Farm—a kitchen composter made from a recycling bin filled with dirt, biodegradable household trash, and a hundred worms. She said she liked the way Dad sat off to the side of me holding his toolbox ("Just in case Old Bessie throws a rod—or a worm, as the case may be.") It showed, she'd said later, after the cameras were off, her hand on my shoulder, that he didn't mind letting someone else be in the spotlight. "You seem so comfortable with yourself. Most guys don't like being behind the scenes," she'd said. "What's your secret?" And then she gave him her phone number.

But now it was April and there was no time to lose. I wanted my dad to propose before summer, before too much time passed.

"Dad?" I was lying on the floor watching TV at his apartment in the new Willow Landing housing development, where I was visiting for the weekend. Over on the couch, he looked up from his sewing; he was mending a tablecloth my mother had let him take after that day in February when she told him he was too selfish to live with other people. She said he was an immature boy who got married before he knew his ass from a hole in the ground and that he'd probably be happy to have one empty affair after another for the rest of his life. "Do you like Darla?" I said. "I mean a whole lot?"

"Yes, I like her," he said, looking at me over the granny glasses he wore for close-up work. I smiled. See? I imagined saying to my mother.

Just then, what I had been hoping for happened: she appeared on the TV, in an ad for the news. Darla Starling. She was interviewing some housewives who were picketing the Mountainside Gentlemen's Club that was between Smoky Ordinary and Haymarket. She stood in an empty gravel parking lot beside a hunched white building with no windows, the sun sparkling off the buttons on her suit. The woman next to her carried a sign that read *Gentlemen? Ha!,* and when Darla asked her about it, the woman said, "They should change the name to something more accurate. Like The Mountainside Simpletons or The Mountainside Booby-Peekers." Then the woman craned her pretty mermaid face into the camera and said, "Do you hear that, Todd?"

Dad clicked his tongue and shook his head. "You're in it up to your neck, Todd," he said to the TV.

The camera focused on Darla. "Will this establishment rise to the challenge?" she said. "We'll have the story at eleven."

I watched Dad's face for some sign; he didn't get that look, like he'd forgotten to turn off the iron, the way people in love did on TV. I ran into the kitchen for one of the juice boxes I'd brought. I was getting sweaty under the arms. What if he wouldn't get engaged? Then, how would my mother ever see that he wasn't selfish and give him a second chance? I straightened up. No. There was no other way. My best friend, Zack Miller, had told me once that old people got gushy and romantic at bowling alleys because they made them think about Doris Day and certain dead presidents and because games with turn-taking always led to people sitting on each other's laps. So, tonight, I had made Dad promise to take Darla and me to the Bowl America. Tonight. Tonight. I took a deep breath.

Right then, I noticed that some woman, someone named "Lisa" had left her number on a sticky note on the kitchen table. The handwriting was wild and looped, and there was a lopsided heart around the number. I crumpled it up and stuffed it deep into the trash can.

"What are you doing?" Dad called.

"Nothing," I said, hurrying back into the living room. I busied myself inspecting his one sickly houseplant for fungi and growths. Maybe Lisa was a customer from McCarty's Outdoor Power Equipment and Repair, where Dad was the manager; or maybe she was a lonely little old lady who wore a fuzzy pink hat and made friends with everyone. Either way, Dad could do without her.

I eyed the clock. "Where's Darla?" I said. "Do you think she's coming?"

"She probably got caught in traffic." He glanced at the clock. "Or maybe—" He yawned and crinkled his nose. "—Maybe she got so worked up about coming to see me, she had to pull off the road and collect herself." He winked at me as if he was joking, but I hoped maybe he was pining. Sometimes Darla didn't call him at the times she said she would, and once, she forgot about a dinner date at The Black-Eyed Pea. Dad had let me order my favorite cheesy rice anyway, and he laughed about the shoe being on the other foot, waving his feet in the air so much as he did that the waitress came over and asked if he was trying to get her attention.

"Aren't you going to get ready?" I said, thinking of the hour my mother had spent drinking wine and dancing around the living room before her date with the vice principal of Smoky Ordinary High School the week before—her first date since the breakup. I had asked her a stream of questions as she put on her makeup, but she brushed them all off. She said the date wasn't anything heavy, nothing that could lead to some difficult thing like marriage.

"I don't know. I guess so," Dad said, looking down at his worn jeans and the Caffeine O.D. T-shirt he'd gotten free after twenty burritos and coffee refills at the HandiMart.

He held the tablecloth up for both of us to inspect; he'd been fixing a tear so that he could have Darla over for a romantic dinner. They had a bet about whether he could cook, because all that was ever in his fridge was beer and half a jar of spaghetti sauce. Light speckled through five or six moth holes. "Shit," he said under his breath. "Well, that's what I get for not being a rich snob with a cedar chest." He looked defeated, like he had been tricked somehow.

When the phone rang, Dad said, "Can you get that, Claire?" He had the needle in his hand again and the end of the thread in his mouth. I wondered then if that thread had been my mother's, too, and I thought about Darla marrying my dad and using it like it was hers. Even though I liked Darla, I didn't like the idea of her holding that thread between her thumb and forefinger, the way I held horseflies I caught near the water fountain at school, studying them, trying to figure out where they'd been and what their baby pictures would look like if horseflies had baby pictures. The difference was, I knew how to hold a horsefly without getting bitten; I suspected Darla would stick herself in the thumb with the needle.

"Claire?" Dad said as the phone kept ringing, and I jumped up from the floor.

I answered and it wasn't Darla; it was Zack Miller, calling for the third time to tell me that certain girls at school hated me.

"Why?" I asked this time, though I didn't exactly want to know. Zack, my best friend since third grade, had recently begun to take delight in telling me bad things. He told me I had bad breath and that my pants were too short and that he could tell by looking at me that I was going to go blind someday and other things. I didn't like it, but I took it. We had a peculiar best-friendship.

"They say you have worms in your hair," he told me. "And underneath your clothes, you don't have skin—just worms. What do you think of that?"

"Those girls are stupid," I said. "Worms couldn't live in hair or on skin." Zack laughed. He liked it when I was scientific. And usually he liked to find out about nature and chemicals and things like that as much as I did.

Just last summer, Zack and I had spent two whole days trying to videotape caps exploding. I had the idea that if we filmed in the dark, we'd see the explosion better.

We sneaked down the rickety wooden steps into Zack's basement, which was dark except for a dim circle of light near the naked bulb that hung from the rafters. It smelled down there like the cat litter box and like mold and like firewood.

"Here goes," Zack had said. I knelt down close to Zack's blond head with the camera and used the stripes of his blue and orange shirt to focus and then he started smashing caps on the concrete floor with a hammer. I caught a quick sight of my own knobby legs and part of my favorite denim shorts with the zipper pockets, and the camera shook with the sound of the first cap pops, like tiny versions of the gun shots on the police show we always watched together. Then, from a dark corner, the cat yowled and raced between Zack's legs. We both yelled and Zack reeled back, flinging the hammer, delivering an impossible direct hit on the light bulb. "Incoming!" he shouted. We covered our heads as shards of glass tinkled on the concrete and the hammer clanged down.

Suddenly, it was very dark and very quiet.

"I think I have glass in my eyeballs," I said. We both liked the word "eyeballs" and said it whenever we could.

"C'mon." Zack took my hand in his and it was soft, but a little bit gritty from the caps. I could see nothing but had a clear picture in my head of his hand with its small fingers and nubby fingernails. We sat on the steps in the dark and held hands for a little while, something we had never done before.

But things had changed since then. Lately, he liked to say mean things to me, like he couldn't help himself, like he was possessed by an alien. The things he told me the girls had said didn't hurt my feelings too badly, though, because I didn't have many girl friends and didn't understand the things they talked about when they gathered on the blacktop

110

at recess. I liked doing things—digging for arrowheads or inspecting patches of clover with my magnifying glass—not talking about boys or clothes or telling secrets.

"They're probably jealous," Zack was saying to me on the phone. "Jealous because Jeremy Turner likes you."

"No, he doesn't," I said.

"Yes, he does. He told me."

"Jeremy Turner is gross," I said. I didn't mean what I said, but I wanted Zack to know I didn't like Jeremy that way. Jeremy Turner was a new kid from Reno, and he had curly blond hair and brown eyes and he wore flannel shirts every day. He was more mature than most everyone else and smoked cigarettes in the woods at recess with some older boys. Sometimes, he sat near me at lunch and I played paper football with him. But that didn't mean he liked me. I was skinny, I had dull brown hair, and I had just started wearing a bra, though I didn't need one yet. I had never had a boyfriend. I didn't want one because that meant I couldn't pay attention to anything else.

"Want to come over tonight?" Zack said. "My parents are going out. We can spy on my brother and his girlfriend."

"Can't. Dad and Darla and me are going to the bowling alley." I glanced at the couch where my dad had been sitting a second before. "He's in the bathroom now," I said. "Smelling up the place with aftershave." I wondered what Zack would say if Darla and my dad got engaged—maybe that Darla might kill my dad just like the woman in the TV movie Black Widow killed the men she got involved with. Or maybe that I should make my room off limits to her so that they wouldn't make out in there while I was over at my mom's. He always told me that adults made out every second of the day that kids weren't around, but I didn't know if I believed him. I thought maybe the only times my parents had kissed a lot was at Christmas and after scary movies.

But Zack didn't seem to guess that anything was going on at my dad's, the way I thought he might, the way I sort of wanted him to. "Maybe I can get my brother to drive me to the bowling alley," he said.

We got off the phone, and I went out on the balcony behind Dad's apartment to wait for the 5:45 commuter train while Dad got ready to go. I sat on one of the white plastic chairs from K-Mart, and my cat Bandit, who always came along on visits, pushed the door and came out behind me. His gray fur shone in the pinkish light and his yellow eyes glowed. I wished my eyes glowed like that. I imagined that my dad would look at them and say, "Oh, man. Your eyes are glowing." And then he would be hypnotized and do whatever I told him to. I reached out my hand and Bandit rubbed against my legs and walked through them in a figure eight.

I liked to watch the trains that went through the scrubby field beyond the balcony—the way they rumbled past, disturbing Twinkie wrappers and paper toilet seats and newspapers that rested on the yellow grass. The afternoon trains were better because the sun lit up the people inside and I could see how fast the train was going by the way their heads whooshed past. I liked to study those people, see them reading newspapers, talking, or staring back at me—a dark-headed figure with her legs propped up on the railing. But today, I wanted to imagine myself in the train with them, drinking coffee and looking out the window, traveling west, a mysterious stranger, like in *Moonraker*, a James Bond movie I'd seen on cable. A person like that had glamorous, interesting problems and he didn't need any help fixing them.

"Are you ready?" Dad said from inside. He gazed into the mirror over the brown and tan couch in the living room and tucked his dark green shirt into his slacks.

"I'm just going to wear this," I said as I walked inside, and I gestured to my jeans and my T-shirt with the butterfly on the front. Dad started to say something about my clothes but then stopped and said never mind.

The railroad crossing bell started to ring then. Bandit scrambled in from the balcony as the train's rumbling grew closer and the apartment began to shake, including the mirror that Dad and I stood in front of. It showed a blurry image of our two dark heads, and we almost looked like Mom and Dad there instead of me and Dad. But Mom was at the Smoky Ordinary High School production of *Nunsense* with the vice principal. I knew that. She told me she wasn't the same person anymore, but I didn't think she looked any different. It was just that she had started going on long walks and to painting classes, and she cried more often. She said things to me like, "Love is a creature with two heads," and "How about if you and me become best friends? Can we do that?"

When Darla finally showed up a few minutes later, she apologized her way toward my dad and they kissed. I had forgotten how much I liked to look at her—she had a turned-up nose and green eyes decorated with mauve eye shadow, and thick sandy hair that she wore loose on her shoulders when she was with us. On TV, she wore her hair in a bun or a twist because she was twenty-nine and the station wanted her to look more serious and grown up.

"So are we going or what?" she said and tugged us both out of the apartment by our sleeves.

We drove straight down Route 29, Jefferson Street, and Darla talked to Dad about the picketing housewife, who she called "a real go-getter" and "a sweetheart," and Dad nodded and said, "How about that." I sat in the back eating a Lifesaver Darla had given me from her purse. The leaves on the pear trees that lined the streets of Smoky Ordinary were almost all grown in, except they were still yellow-green. Baby leaves. The shops had put out their summer awnings, blue and white, and it was still so light out and so warm that an old couple sat eating ice cream cones on a bench that commemorated some sort of massacre. I thought about one time the summer before when my mom, dad, and I got ice cream cones. My dad had gotten so angry about something my mother said that he threw his in the trash.

Just then, Darla wrestled out of her jacket, rolled up her sleeves, and stuck her hand into the fresh air. My dad looked at her and then turned on my favorite radio station instead of the oldies he normally listened to. I imagined Darla was my mother, and the three of us were a family. I pictured us all eating ice cream cones and singing like the Von Trapps. But then I felt guilty and I put my face closer to the open window and tried to look down at the daffodils that lined the street.

At the Bowl America out by the interstate, the wooden sound of pins crashing was louder than I remembered from the last time I'd been there with Dad, who bet me my allowance but wouldn't take it when he won. Just inside, I saw Jeremy Turner and his friends playing ancient video games like *Mortal Kombat* and *Slayer* in a dark corner by the door. I could feel my face get hot when they all saw me and Jeremy waved. I smiled, but waved only slightly because I didn't want my dad or Darla to notice.

As we cleared the entryway, we arrived at the center of fifteen or twenty blue-trimmed shiny wooden lanes with red seats around the scoring tables. Fluorescent lights hung from the rafters just like in the gym at school, but people weren't all wearing yellow shirts and maroon shorts, so they didn't look nearly as weird and pasty. Also, there was a colorful banner that read "Saturday is Family Day! Mom, Dad, Bobby, and Sis all bowl for $8!" I wondered if Dad and Darla got the hint.

We went down to the lane we were assigned, number 10, and we all changed shoes on the wooden benches. We bowled then for about an hour; I threw so many gutter balls that my dad put up the bumpers. My wrist and fingers got sore, but I liked the rumbling I felt in my chest from so many balls and pins crashing together on the wood all around us.

It was going pretty well. In the eighth frame of the third game, Dad got a strike and then spiked an imaginary football before strutting back to his seat. Darla laughed, like she thought it was funny, not like she thought he was sort of a moron. And that was good. I'd heard once on CNN that scientists believed laughter produced a chemical effect in the brain that made people want to spend more time together.

But then, as he walked back toward us, Dad glanced over our heads toward the door, and his eyes got very big. "I'll be right back," he said. He trotted over to a woman in a yellow dress who was holding hands with a small boy. The woman grinned when she saw him and started to reach out, but then, when he started hustling her back outside, she looked scared and sad.

Darla was sitting beside me on the bench. When I turned back around, our faces were inches apart. She had been watching, too.

"That's one of his customers," I said.

"I don't think so," she told me and she looked very serious. I remembered how Dad had told me that Darla had a boyfriend until last year and they'd been together for a long, long time. But he got very sad and tried to kill himself and now he lived in Florida with his parents.

"Do you like my dad?" I said.

"Yes, I do," she said quietly. Then she seemed almost to be talking to herself. "He's very charming," she said. "Very charming indeed."

"My dad likes you, too," I said. "He talks about you a lot."

She stopped and looked at me strangely and then squeezed my shoulder. "You're sweet," she said. We were both quiet for a moment then. "Claire, let me ask you something," she said. "Do you want to go to college?"

I nodded. "My mom says she'll drag me through a hedge backwards if I don't go."

Darla laughed. "Let me tell you something about what it means to be an educated woman, okay?"

I nodded and scooted closer.

"Eventually," she said, "you will get sick and tired of how wishy-washy, how spineless professional men are. And you'll think the answer is to go out with someone who's a bit more...salt of the earth." She put her hand on my shoulder. "Remember what I'm about to tell you, Claire: this is not the answer."

"Oh," I said, pretending to have a revelation, but not really knowing what she was talking about. She patted my shoulder.

When my dad came back, Darla got up to go to the restroom. She looked over her shoulder as she walked away and smiled sort of like she did at the end of the news. Sometimes, I wanted to put my hands on her face to make sure she was real even though I knew she was. I wondered if Dad was afraid she'd disappear into that second of black screen between her program and the commercials and he'd have to be alone, which is how my mom told me he'd end up someday.

"Why don't you get a snack?" He dug in his pocket and then handed me five dollars from his wallet.

It wasn't normal for Dad to give me money like that, and I wasn't quite sure what to spend it on. At the snack bar, I stood back and read the menu on the wall, trying not to notice Jeremy Turner, who was over at the bar trying to buy cigarettes, arguing with a woman that he was old enough. I ordered popcorn and a Coke, paid for them, and then went over to the condiments area to get some napkins.

Over my shoulder, a hand reached down into my popcorn. Zack's hand. He helped himself to my popcorn. "Needs salt," he said, leaning against the counter, crunching loudly, like he was pleased with himself for being so sneaky.

"I don't like salt," I told him, and ate a handful myself to prove the point. "How long have you been here?"

"A while," he said. "I've been playing *Slayer* with Jeremy. He has the hots for you. He thinks about you at the strangest times, if you know what I mean."

"What are you talking about?"

"If you don't know, I'm not saying."

"Whatever. I don't care," I said.

"That's not what he thinks. He thinks you're in love with him."

"Why does he think that?"

"Because that's what I told him."

"Zack! What'd you do that for?" I looked right into Zack's eyes then and he moved his face even closer to mine.

"Well, why not? Isn't it true?"

"No! You know it isn't." I stopped for a second, waving my hands, looking for more words. "Why can't you just be nice to me?"

He fumbled with the strings from his sweatshirt hood and stepped back and looked away for a second like he was waiting for someone. "What about you?" he said, keeping his eyes on the strings around his fingers. "You spend all your time by yourself or else flicking the football with Jeremy Turner. You wander around in the grass at recess looking for bugs like there's nobody else there. You draw pictures at lunch and don't talk."

"I do not," I said. But I knew he was right.

"I wish I was finished with school forever, like my brother." Zack wiped his forehead with the back of his hand, which trembled a little.

"But you don't care." He looked at me again, but coolly, as if he might do another mean thing. "You don't care."

"What are you talking about? I do care," I said and I meant it, but all I could think about was what he'd said about me. I thought how it was true that I'd ignored Zack at recess, but not the way he thought. At those times, it seemed like I didn't have any thoughts at all. Or maybe like my head was so full of thoughts I couldn't think.

I looked over at my dad, who had his arm draped around Darla's shoulder and was gesturing with his other hand while he talked. Her eyes stared away from him, toward a group of people at another lane.

"Time to go hang with your dad, right?" Zack sighed. "I guess I'll see you around," he said and marched back to Jeremy and his friends, who were sitting on the floor by the video games and laughing. None of them had any cigarettes. I had my mouth open as if I might think of what to say and call Zack back.

When I wandered over to Lane 10, Darla was changing her shoes. "You about ready to go?" she said and then walked away, toward the shoe return.

Dad took a sip of my Coke, but I pulled the cup away from him. "What's wrong with you?" I said. "Why don't you stop messing everything up!"

"Maybe for your next science project, Claire, you can figure out a way for people to control their feelings." He clenched his jaw and muscles moved in his forehead. "Just put your shoes on," he said and walked toward where Darla was waiting by the door.

I glanced away, embarrassed, and caught sight of Zack in his baggy jeans, leaning hard against the *Heavy Metal* pinball machine, as if it might float away. I wondered if I could control the feeling of dread I had about making him understand how I liked him and the feeling of joy I had from seeing, whenever we hadn't been around each other for a while, the cowlick that parted his hair over his right eye. Then, just out of habit, I looked down, wanting to escape, wanting to see wild strawberries, crab grass, honeysuckle, a June bug, aphids, something. But all I saw on the polished floorboards were my own feet in borrowed shoes, red and blue, dusty, and reminding me of other people.

Strike Anywhere

When Rochelle refers to your brother Scott as "Sparks," which is his prison name, you feel certain you've lost her. She perches on the arm of your sofa, slender ankles crossed just below the hem of her sheer blue dress, neck craned toward Scott, who traipses through your off-white living room in work boots. He has been living with you for three months. You cannot, at this moment, remember the last time you spoke to him.

"Hey, Sparks," Rochelle says sweetly. Just like that— "Hey, Sparks." Her hands wring the playbill from *Damn Yankees*, which you and she have just gone to see at the Lazy Susan Dinner Theatre with Carl Summers from the office and his wife Penny. Rochelle likes to attend matinees and also to clip coupons and shop at discount stores. Never thrift stores. "I'm afraid I'll see something of mine. And it would be too weird. Like I was dead or something."

You didn't want to get involved with anyone after your wife, Jody, left six months ago, but the thing with Rochelle just sort of happened at a happy hour one day after work. You and Carl Summers were celebrating the yearly salary increase at your accounting firm, Duff & Beckman, and you spilled red wine spritzer on Rochelle's bare lower leg. Impulsively, you tried to brush it off with your hand. Rochelle giggled. "Shouldn't we at least have dinner first?"

"You've got a deal," you said and bent down and dabbed at her shapely calf, imagining what you would know for certain later—the taste of it, the smell of it. Rochelle fills your days with electric and plaguing daydreams and some of your nights with the kind of passion you once had with Jody. You aren't sure when, during the last part of your nine-year marriage, you realized it was gone. Rochelle fills an empty space you had not understood as emptiness, a space you dismissed as a temporary malaise, a rut, an abiding bad mood. Or, at least, she could fill it. If only you could ever be sure of her feelings for you.

Flann

But now. Now, she has referred to your brother Scott as "Sparks,"
even though you've never called him that. It's a nickname that Scott
got the first time he was in prison, because he smuggled cigarettes and
matches to the other inmates. Why would Rochelle use that name?
True, most of the people who phone for Scott, those who aren't parole
officers, ask for "Sparks." (You always respond deliberately, "I'll be
happy to give Scott a message" or "Yes, Scott's right here. Let me put
him on." How will your brother, your older brother at that, ever get a
salaried job or an apartment or simply refrain from thievery if he goes
by a name like Sparks?) But Rochelle never answers your phone, and
Scott rarely has friends over. Instead of looking at want ads or dealing with the questions you might ask about what he's been doing since
April, when he got out, he typically spends his evenings at a bar called
The El Corazon Disco Lounge, with God knows who.

As you see it, the only way Rochelle would know that name, "Sparks,"
is if she's been spending time with Scott that you don't know about.
Right? you ask yourself.

How many times, in your teenage years, did you hear girls speak to
Scott, in that way Rochelle just did, heads lowered, eyes raised win-
somely, as if to say, "You. You alone have the power to hurt me." It
isn't that you mind, but you wonder sometimes, in a scientific sense,
why girls or women, even your wife, have never spoken to you that
way. Perhaps you aren't rugged or daring enough. But that also means
that you're not a risk to end up in prison, and shouldn't that be attractive? Or maybe (you cringe to think it) your wife was right that you
ask too many questions and you're too literal, too precise. You take the
mystery and fun out of everything: ballroom dancing lessons, dinner
conversation, miniature golf, sex. Thinking of Jody's furious litanies,
you can picture the way her freckled nose used to flatten slightly when
she was angry.

There wasn't a trace of anger on the day that she told you she wanted
to split up, though. "I'm just not excited anymore," she had said and
could not seem to explain further. You wanted to know: since she
didn't know her present potential for excitement, how could she accu-
rately assess her present level? And how could you be the sole source
of her discontent? Maybe part of it was the fact that the interior design
studio where she worked making appointments had lost nearly everything in a flood, and she'd been furloughed indefinitely. And surely
part of her pain was due to the fact that her aunt, Lucille, had died in a
flukey subway accident in New York City. But these suggestions only

120

caused Jody to shake her head like she was sorry for you. It was, you often think as you drive home to Willow Landing, your new apartment complex just off I-66, unjust, short-sighted, and cowardly on her part. But her failure doesn't grant you any vindictive, creative anger. Most of the time, you feel Jody's absence keenly. It's like getting used to the loss of an arm or a leg; every minute of the day, you're off balance.

"Do you want to go out to eat?" you say now to Rochelle, pretending still to be occupied with the coffee maker in the kitchen. But you've seen and you've heard, and you lean against the kitchen doorway, just out of her sight.

"Huh?" she says, smiling at Scott, who has patted her on the shoulder as he passes.

"Come out to eat with me," you say. "I'll take you to that crab house up in Alexandria." You sip your coffee, and look out the second-story kitchen window at several young guys who are lighting charcoal and listening to the Stones and laughing into their beers; the sun is dying in the little green courtyard.

"I can't," Rochelle says. "I'm eating with Trish." She plucks her purse from the end-table and straps it across her shoulder. "You have time to take me home?"

You try to think of something that would make her stay. There is a prickly sense somewhere—your arm hairs? your stomach?—that you will maybe suffocate or drown if she's gone.

But you take her home anyway (what choice do you have?), and you neither suffocate nor drown, though your breathing is shallow, labored. You feel in your lungs the humid Virginia air, perfumed with gardenia, as you watch Rochelle disappear into her little brown townhouse, giving you an easy wave as she shuts the door. You are not satisfied with the wave you give back, and you replay it on your way home. Stiff, uptight. No wonder she's falling for Scott.

You redouble your efforts. The next morning (it's Sunday), you call her and suggest that the two of you spend the day on Lake Iroquois in Carl Summers' boat, the S.S. Partycruiser, a motorized affair made up mostly of bamboo, strings of lights, and inflatable mascots. You hope the message is clear: You can be a fun guy. As fun as the next guy. Particularly if the next guy is Scott.

"I can't, hon," she says. "I have to write up some copy before to-morrow. But you go. I'll channel you out there on the lake." Rochelle writes ads for a company that markets fishing lures. She created the firm's slogan: "Fish find us alluring!"

"Okay," you say. "That's cool. Whatever. We'll do it another time." You hope you sound laid back. You even try to convince yourself that you are: What's the big deal? you say to yourself. She's just a chick. It's just a boat. You think using the word chick will make you feel more in control, the way Scott takes control of conversations with strangers by calling them "Chief" in a joking, dismissive way. But chick isn't the same as chief, and thinking isn't the same as speaking, and you can't dismiss any of your fear about Rochelle.

But then, when you get off the phone, you collect yourself. Everything really is okay. Rochelle is essentially doing homework. You love your brother. You love your brother. You love your brother.

He comes into the kitchen, where you are erect at the table, tapping a pen on the front page of the paper, where there is a photo of people digging bodies out of earthquake rubble.

"Hey," Scott says and pours himself a bowl of chocolate cereal. He sits down across from you and shovels the brown bits into his mouth, milk showering back into the bowl. "I'm thinking of becoming a bartender," he says, crunching. He glances at you for a reaction. You say nothing, keep tapping. "The money's good and there's this school at night. It only takes six weeks."

He's waiting. Bartender? After he went to prison for a bar fight that got way too serious. You feel disgusted, but then you think: What would I like him to do? Maybe join the Peace Corps and move to Angola. Why is he here? To get back on his feet, to find work. Did you ever want him here? Why did you invite him? You seem to recollect some tenderness upon seeing him walk out of the prison wearing the clothes he went in with three years before—khaki pants and a green tennis shirt—what he called his "judge clothes." But also there is the fact that your mother is long dead and your father died just last year, shot and killed when someone held up his restaurant. Where else was Scott to go? You should be glad that Scott wants to be a bartender. It means he'll move out, have his own money. You can come sleep on his sofa and steal his girlfriend. You must make sure he becomes a bartender.

"I've always wanted to be a bartender, too," you say. "It's all night classes, you're telling me? Let's do it together. It'll be fun. Like old times."

Of course, with the two of you, there are no old times. You and Scott worked throughout your childhoods and teenaged years in your father's restaurant up in Maryland where you grew up. Your father allowed no speaking in the kitchen. "Keep your mind where it belongs," he'd say.

"People can taste it if you're not paying attention." To this day, though it isn't what your father meant, you imagine that a nasty metallic flavor materializes on others' tongues whenever you are inattentive. It is unnerving to you when your boss licks his lips.

You write a check and Scott enrolls the two of you in the Bartender's Academy forty-five minutes up the interstate in Washington, DC. During the Monday and Wednesday evening classes, you learn how to make Rusty Nails, Slippery Nipples, Fuzzy Navels. You learn how to make the liquor almost tasteless in the drinks. You learn that men are better customers than women. "Women will nurse their drinks. But men are self-destructive," the teacher says. He goes on to make one of his witty social commentaries. "Men destroy themselves. Whereas women like to let others pitch in and help." Everyone laughs, but you don't really have any idea what he's talking about.

While the teacher rambles through another bit of liquor philosophy—demonstrating, you should recognize, how to keep a barroom full of happy people glad to order more—your mind drifts and you think of your mother and the cancer that killed her when you were ten. You remember your father carrying her to the bathroom. You were jealous because he had told you the year before that you were a big boy and big boys didn't get carried around. They walked on their own two feet. You thought maybe your father loved your mother more than he loved you. Once, you even sneaked into their bathroom and put the toilet lid down, just to make things more difficult. It was probably your father's smoking that made her sick, but at the time you thought it was her hateful desire to have your father all to herself.

At least you and Jody didn't do that, you didn't kill each other, inadvertently or otherwise. The divorce was actually amiable; neither of you spoke much while you divided up photos, dishes, towels, though Jody cried a little. She even let you hold her and stroke her coppery hair and you think now that you should have seen it coming, that she had tried to tell you that you had become distant and that you weren't the same fun-loving guy who fake proposed to her on the first date. Maybe she was right that you became a different person after your father died, and that she could see you better than you could see yourself.

You miss her. Right there in bartending class, you miss her. The feeling passes through you, and there's an urgency, as if maybe you need to use the restroom. You don't actually need to, but you leave anyway, go out to the fluorescent lobby with its blue vinyl couches, and call Jody from the payphone. She answers, her voice light and sleepy, like maybe she's been reading a book, maybe she's wearing a white flannel nightgown with little pink flowers on it. You hang up.

The next day, you quit your job; you don't give any notice at all, just tell your boss and then start packing your things. Carl Summers corners you in your office. "Have you really thought this through?" he says.

"No," you tell him. "But I think that's the point." You pause. "Of course. . . I'm not sure."

What you know for certain is that you never want to see this office again, not the little box of push pins meant to impale phone messages on the wall or the Shroud-of-Turin-shaped water stain on the ceiling.

You start spending your days with Scott. Are you doing all of this just to make sure that he isn't going around with Rochelle? You are objective enough to know that would be a little crazy. You're starting to wonder if you even like Rochelle very much. In restaurants, she stuffs handfuls of napkins and sugar packets into her purse. "What?" she says to you. "They factor this into their overhead." She stares over your shoulder while you're talking as if she's waiting for her real date to show up. Her mind seems to be fixed on some point in the future, and the present is just for passing the time and getting supplies ready. Her highest praise is, "Oooh. Shangri-la!"

It's hard to imagine that Scott would be interested in her. You've begun to realize that he's probably smarter than you. You hate it when you have to alter your perceptions of reality. You wonder how many times they've changed since you were ten. It makes you so tired that you try not to have many significant experiences. And when you have one, you try to play it off like you're not, as if you can fool yourself, which you can—for a while—sometimes.

One day, when you're at the end of a pier fishing in the lake with Scott (it turns out that's how Scott spends a lot of his time), you realize that you are actually going to become a bartender. You like the idea of being tender, of tending to something. You might even buy a bar and call it. . . The Tender Bar. . . or The Meeting Place. Well, you'd call it something. With your bookkeeping skills, you might have a long-lasting place like your father's. You look over your shoulder at Scott. "Why do you think Dad was such a hard ass?" you say.

Scott reels in his line a little, making gentle clicks. "Because things mattered to him," Scott says. "I used to think he was such an asshole and I never wanted to be like he was, about anything. And look how fucked up things got." The clicks of Scott's fishing rod make you think of ideas pulling tight in your brain. You think of Rochelle's fishing lures, how they work in the same way as the things that catch a person by surprise all through life. You can't know until it's too late that something's going to puncture your guts. How can you know that a man who walks into a restaurant with a paper sack is going to shoot you in the head? When you are ten years old and you decide that it is important for things to matter to you, how can you know that they will matter and matter and matter? How can you guess that the worst thing you will do in your life is pretend that they don't?

"What if we call the bar 'Sparks'?" you say. You wiggle your fingers, which have fallen asleep.

"Just so long as no one calls me that anymore," Scott says. "I'm sick to death of it." He lets his line out and then tugs at it. "I didn't know we were getting a bar."

You shrug. He doesn't say anything.

You decide you like the way the midday sun winks on the water, tiny disappearing diamonds.

An Airtight Box

During intermission of the *Tosca* benefit performance, ex-President Clinton, without Hillary, stepped outside the door of his Kennedy Center box, wondering what it would be like if someone shot him, maybe in his good lung, or maybe, if the attacker had lousy aim, even in the groin. He waved and sidled over to the people that had gathered on the other side of the velvet rope. At his first step toward them, the people broke into applause. He shook hands and stood in one place for a good three minutes, something that always made the guys on his Secret Service detail twitchy. Surely a non-lethal gunshot wound—one intended to inflict pain instead of death, which a lot of shooters do, according to the guys—would distract him from the sick, heavy feeling in his chest, like his organs were being squeezed between two pieces of Amazonian timber.

This morning in New York, his doctor's cold stethoscope, pressed hard against the site of last week's surgery, had felt as weighty as a beam. "Well, I've taken a good long gander into the abyss this time, haven't I?" he'd said, and shifted on the exam table, the paper sheet crinkling beneath him. "The bypass wasn't enough? I had to drive by for another look? Well, that's me all over, Doc," he'd explained, laughing, which made his pectoral muscles ache as if he'd bench pressed too much.

"Please don't speak until I'm done with this, Mr. President," the doctor had said.

He nodded. "I always drive by for another look," he'd finished, more quietly. He'd wondered if the sound of his heart racing was as loud to the doctor as it was in his own ears. He winked at his assistant, who was sitting in a green vinyl chair in the corner, talking on her cell phone to her assistant, confirming the arrangements for the flight to Washington and for her pre-session briefing with key Democratic House members.

She didn't acknowledge the president's wink; she said he only winked when he was nervous. She had no patience with nervousness. She covered the mouth piece of the phone and sighed; the president braced himself. But she only said, to the doctor, "Please feel free to tell him to stop being so ridiculous." The sunlight, a little weak and watery, shone on the left side of her face. Her eyes were so blue.

The doctor stood erect, looked at the president's assistant, who was talking on the phone again, and then he looked right at the president's face; the stethoscope still dangled from his neck. The doctor's dark hair was tousled and he was rugged and handsome except for his discolored skin and teeth, which suggested a habit of cigarettes and whiskey, maybe bourbon, and there was something slightly unsettling, wolfish in his unremitting eye contact. The president found this look all too familiar.

"I keep telling you," the doctor said. "This fluid in your lungs, it's rare after the surgery." He spoke with a Carolina accent, but haltingly, like each word was a gumball he had to retrieve from the bottom of a narrow-necked jar. "A nuisance, definitely. I'm sure it's had you wheezing like a bulldog. And when your lung collapsed, it must have scared the holy hellfire out of you. But it really is no big deal. Only a complication from the bypass. The decortication fixed it. No more fluid and no more scar tissue. You'll be a new man in no-time flat. Scout's honor," he said, fumbling to hold up some fingers in a scout-like manner; it was clear he had no idea which ones. Giving up on that particular gesture, he patted the president's shoulder. "You were just unlucky."

Unlucky. The word had stayed with him all day. It had never ever been applied to him before. Ever. Anytime in his life there'd been a whiff of bad luck in the air, he'd ducked it, dodged it, or hosed it down with something that smelled a whole lot sweeter. And as for his accomplishments, no one ever referred to those as luck. The concept of luck was impotent, like an old man. Except now he himself was an old man. Or, at least, nearly.

The Kennedy Center was a low-security crowd, all the DC professionals and key Democrats you could squeeze into one orchestra hall. It was a little boring, if the president was honest with himself. There was no work to do here.

When he spotted the woman on the other side of the velvet rope—a statuesque girl, really, with long, dark hair, shiny as an oil slick—he drifted over as if he was heading that direction anyway, shaking hands, patting children's heads. He wasn't thinking of what was coming next. He was just looking, just having a look.

"How are you? How you folks doing?" he said. "Good to see you."

"Nothing's been the same since you left," complained a heavyset woman in thick glasses that made her eyes look like small brown fish.

"You're not kidding," he said. "I miss all that free stationery." He got a laugh from more than just the woman. "And no one plays music when I walk into a room anymore. It's so dang quiet. Even Sam ignores me." He looked over at the head honcho of his Secret Service detail, who was standing beside the entrance to the box in that military "at ease" position, not quite right with the crisp dark suit or the crow's feet around his eyes. He was more Dirty Harry than GI Joe. "Isn't that right, Sam?"

Sam didn't respond, just kept scanning the middle distance as if the president hadn't spoken. After a beat, the agent looked at his watch with just a trace of boredom. The crowd erupted with laughter. Bill looked at them as if to say, Do you see what I have to put up with?

He and Sam had been perfecting this gag for five years. This was version one. In version two, Sam said, "Yes, sir, ignoring you completely, sir," which the crowds always found equally funny. The gag worked, he thought, because no one expected the Secret Service guys to be up for a laugh. They saw the guys as inhuman, could almost sense the qualities different from themselves—the better-than 20/20 vision the guys were required to have or the fact that they were all world-class, precise-to-a-hair, bona fide marksmen. Luck, the president thought, I've got your luck.

The girl was tall, alabaster-skinned, maybe thirty-one or thirty-two, with a dazzling and mischievous smile. She hovered on the edge of the crowd, not quite one of them, not quite waiting to meet him. With a quick glance over the heads of the people to his left, the president noted her snug black turtleneck, the two less attractive, shorter friends pulling her forward toward the rope, the resigned, amused roll of her eyes.

He took his time, shook more hands, chatted with a lady from Hot Coffee, Mississippi, and signed her program. But without looking, he kept tabs on the girl, took as long as he could to get to her; in his experience, the longer people waited for something, the more attachment they developed to that thing. Of course, in this case, it meant that he himself was waiting, as well.

When he finally stood in front of her, she had murky green eyes and a firm dry handshake that sent tingles up his arm, not like the clammy limp numbers he got from most members of the public. Her friends squealed, but she didn't. Her eyes simply opened a little bit wider, and one corner of her mouth started to rise, in the beginning of what could be a smile. In that instant, he pictured his daughter's imploring face, much younger than it was now. "Promise me, Daddy. No more." It was a promise he hadn't been particularly apt at keeping. There had been a few slip-ups. But since Hillary had won office, he'd been the model of restraint. Hillary still yelled at him just as much. He still secretly liked it.

He knew he shouldn't do what he was about to do, he knew it was bad, but he caught Sam's eye nonetheless and gave him the nod, a nod he hadn't given since he didn't know when. This was exactly the sort of abuse of his security detail that he had always been accused of in Washington, but Sam understood. Sam was in his third marriage and also had a girlfriend who worked in a café on Capitol Hill. That girlfriend was a regulations and security breach all by herself, even if he never told her who he worked for; Sam would be fired in an instant if Bill mentioned it. "Hey, we are who we are," Sam was fond of saying with a shrug. "Guys who live big and fuck big."

After that, sitting in the box next to Hillary's empty seat, the president felt a little better, but he had trouble concentrating through the rest of the Puccini. The president counted the number of faces that turned to look at his reaction when Tosca's lover was being killed: 32. He scanned the crowd for the girl and her friends, but he couldn't make them out. Well, beauty didn't necessarily correlate with money. She might be in the balcony.

As soon as the performance ended, he hurried down a back stairwell, skipping the Kennedy Center's Hall of Presidents, with its familiar red carpet, massive chandeliers, and one last crowd to greet. Outside, he leaned toward Sam, who whispered her name into his ear: "Sarah Heston." The president veritably leapt into his limousine, hardly noticing the nip of the November air.

And there she was; she was sipping champagne and flipping through the president's copy of *Rolling Stone*. Good old Sam. The president's motorcade—less conspicuous than when he was in office, just two tan SUVs and his black stretch Lincoln—headed up the ramp out of the parking garage, toward the Watergate Hotel, just one block away.

"Your goon said my friends couldn't come," she said, blinking. "Why is that?"

"Sarah," the president said. "Is it okay if I call you Sarah?" He knew it was okay. This was simply a tactic he'd learned to allow himself a moment's thought and to make people feel especially respected, if the occasion warranted. The car smelled faintly of pineapple—he just knew it was her hair, her long dark hair, which spilled in a haphazard fashion over the fur-trimmed collar of her coat. "You intrigue me, Sarah."

"Well, if that will get me a ride home, fine. But I'm not going to sleep with you."

"You're direct," the president said. "That's an excellent quality."

"Thanks. Did you hear what I said? That I'm not going to sleep with you?"

"How about I give you a personal tour of my suite at the Watergate?"

"No, thanks."

He looked at her earnestly and tried his fail-safe line, the one that always, always worked: "I've made a lot of mistakes, Sarah. I won't say I haven't."

"Have you read this article about The Hooks? I think they're a British band. Do you know them?"

"All right," he sighed. "Where do you live?"

It had to be Smoky Ordinary, didn't it? Some tiny place beyond the farthest away Virginia suburb the president could even name. He gave his driver her address and got comfortable in the seat. He hated riding backwards. Perhaps she hadn't realized that she was sitting on his side of the car. He should have sat next to her. What was he thinking? He was rusty, that was all. He had at least an hour to rescue the situation. He had seduced a nation once upon a time. Bill, get yourself together. Get your head back in the game.

He looked out the window at the Potomac, at the way the lights and fine rain made the surface sparkle. "I miss DC," he said. "The North doesn't suit me." Then he looked at Sarah again, her face intermittently lit up by the city outside. She wore hardly any makeup and her creamy skin was unlined; yet she didn't have a baby face. Up close, it was hard to guess within ten years how old she was. "What do you do for a living?" he asked. He laughed, remembering something he was once told. "That's the big question DC people ask each other when they first meet, right? What do you do?"

"I'm a photographer," she said. "This isn't bad, by the way," she said, pouring him a glass of champagne. "And I'm not 'DC people.' I'm from Virginia."

What was with this girl? No one from Northern Virginia ever owned up to living there, unless pressed. He took the glass from her. He wasn't supposed to drink. But what the hell. It was going to be a long night. "Thank you, my dear. Cheers." He drained it in a single long swallow, and passed it to her to refill.

"Cheers," she said.

They were quiet for a while after that. Sarah wasn't speechless in a doe-eyed way. She didn't look at him adoringly, or fearfully, with her mouth open a little as if willing words to come out. Instead, she flipped through the magazine as if she were at the hairdresser, her long legs crossed at the knee in a relaxed fashion and the top one bouncing a little, her sparkly high-heeled shoe peeking out from under the hem of her slacks.

"What?" she finally said, smacking her palms onto the pages on her lap.

"I'm sorry?"

"Why do you keep staring at me?"

The president leaned against the window and sighed. He wondered if Hillary was still in that emergency session of Congress. If the country was going to go to war, he would get a call soon. He could picture the fullness of Hillary's mouth when she was thinking, the intensity of her blue, blue eyes. Was she speaking right now, that room full of suits under the spell of her no-nonsense voice? He could imagine her saying the words they had penned together earlier, in a conference call: "Democracy does not end with a constitution and the right to vote. It is a never-ending struggle that we must grapple with every day." He let the words roll around in his head. Yes, a struggle, a carefully orchestrated effort. Not something that could exist by accident. God, it was exciting when the two of them worked together. His wife had the sexiest, sharpest mind he'd ever encountered. Screw the press and all their insinuations about divorce—their love, unorthodox as it was, had done things for the country that historians would still be discovering decades from now.

The lamp above Sarah's head cast a gauzy glow around her. It flickered for a moment, and she set the magazine aside. He blinked, and the limousine's whole cabin seemed to grow dimmer. He felt incredibly tired. He was pretty sure the drugs he was on were incompatible with liquor. He shut his eyes—just a quick snooze, he thought.

When he managed to open his eyes and look out the window again, the limo was cruising down a two-lane highway through some woods. He wasn't sure where he was at first. His arms and legs tingled with sleep. He could see nothing, just blackness, and it was as if he was riding through the hills of Arkansas, his mother's bright red lips twisted into a grimace as she steered the Ford Impala through the darkness. He could almost believe she was at the wheel of the car; he could see the way she would gesture to this girl with the nod of her head. "There's no such thing as a stranger, Billy," she would say. "They're just friends you haven't met yet." She would get out her compact, pat her nose, one wrist steadying the car. "Your problem is, you've been spending too much time with rich people, city people, and Northerners. Sweetie, you talk all the time but you've forgotten how to say anything."

He was aware now that he was rubbing the velour beside him, directly behind the driver's seat, as if checking if his mother was there. The girl was staring out the window. He looked at her, tried to focus. Her dark hair was so beautiful; he desperately wanted to touch it. "So which photographers do you like, Sarah?" he said. "Francois-Marie Banier?"

She made surprised eye contact and then wrinkled her brow. "He photographs celebrities," she said, with a tone that might be reserved for words like landfill or maggots. "He's talented, of course. But can you think of any subject more boring?" She let out a little snorting laugh, surprising herself, and then covering her mouth and laughing for real. Her hand was broad with short natural fingernails and no jewelry; this was a hand that actually did work, he thought. He could imagine Sarah in her darkroom, the wonder in her eyes as images appeared on the paper in her fingertips.

"Bertien Van Manen?" the president tried.

Sarah stopped laughing, her face slack as if he'd slapped her. "You know who she is?"

"Of course. I went to 'Give Me Your Image' in Madrid last summer. It was amazing."

"She's my favorite photographer," Sarah said in a tiny, almost inaudible voice.

Finé.

The girl's eyes stared out the window at the darkness. The president let the quiet remain for a few minutes then, just the sound of the wheels hitting potholes.

"You're a tough nut to crack, Sarah Heston," he said, smiling. He already had her, he knew.

She looked at him thoughtfully. "Well, you see, here's the thing. I was married for three years. His name was Bill, too," she said. "I used to work for a cookbook publisher." She stopped and looked at her fingernails. "I was just there while I got my photography off the ground. And then we met." She bit the nail on her index finger and kept talking. "Only, I didn't know he was married to someone else. Actually, which one of us he married first, I have no idea." She studied the president's face. "I've always wondered: If you marry two people, is that still adultery? Legally, I mean. He's going to hell either way."

He smiled at her and studied her face in return. You never knew with some of the girls he met; they could have stunning figures, dress with impeccable style, and the instant they spoke, they'd become utterly undesirable. Not so with this girl. Her unselfconscious frankness made him want to share in return. Did she know that his own father, William Jefferson Blythe, who died before Bill was born, was rumored to have been a bigamist? Did she know that most people studiously avoided the word adultery in his presence? He wondered for the first time if she was a reporter.

He knew his ice blue eyes would twinkle under the streetlights. He also knew, from years of practice, never to answer the questions he was asked, but the question he wished he had been asked. "I would love to see your photographs, Sarah Heston," he told her. There was no question now. She was ready to melt: finé.

He never went to girls' houses. It was too personal, and much, much too risky. But now he had to find out who the hell she was. Make the whole thing look like a misunderstanding if need be. He'd been reckless, there was no doubt about it. He had no idea who her friends were or how soon they might talk. His heart felt like there was a rope tied around the middle of it. That little pink mouth, the way her nose wrinkled when she was thinking, still looking out the window instead of at him. He knew she would make him laugh or shout—she was that kind of intense. She was either incredibly calculating or one of the most genuine, un-Washington people he'd met in years.

The three-vehicle motorcade drove down the main street of the town, and he could see the reflection of the speeding, shiny cars reflected in the shop windows. There was a hardware store and an old mom-and-pop grocery with a bright pink front. In the town square, there was a statue of a man on a horse—Stonewall Jackson, the president assumed—still facing north, never to retreat. A shaggy, three-legged dog hurried down the sidewalk at a surprising pace. The limo turned and entered a residential area, small white houses with porches and the occasional brick rambler. It reminded him of Hope, his hometown. He halfway expected to see Miss Marie Purkins' School for Little Folks, the squat cinderblock building where his ability to read at the age of four had famously dazzled the staff. It had been his first intoxicating taste of success.

"This is it," Sarah said, pointing. "Stop here."

The driver had already pulled to the curb. He walked around the car and let Sarah out. "You really want to see my photos?" she said, her forehead wrinkled with doubt.

"I do," he said. He smiled. "My guys have to give me the okay, though." His driver shut the door again.

Sam had the president well-trained to wait in the car. He watched two of the agents follow Sam and Sarah into the house, and a few minutes later, Sam appeared. He nodded at the guy positioned next to the president's car door; the agent opened it and waited for the president to get out.

He wasn't sure. Was this a good idea? If she was a reporter he was done for already; he should cut his losses and get out of here. If she'd been wearing a wire, he hadn't said anything overly untoward yet, had he? He replayed the last hour in his mind, imagined Hillary's reaction, her flared nostrils, the flash of her eyes. This image, though, only excited him, a fiery ball in his stomach.

The president got out of the car, walked up the rickety front steps. The rain had stopped, and the air smelled like wet grass and the magnolia tree next to the porch. The tree frogs were chirping. Not a single light was on down the whole block. It was like going back in time to 1949, when he still lived with his grandparents at 117 South Hervey, and his mother had not yet returned from New Orleans with exactly one nursing degree and one abusive husband named Roger. Nowadays, he inked Roger out of most of his memories. He liked to imagine his mother was always the sassy, confident woman she became after his death. He pictured her now coming to the door to greet him, a Tom Collins in her hand and Duke Ellington on the radio.

He hesitated at the door, studying Sam's face for some positive or negative reaction. Sam, however, gave nothing away, and the president stepped over the threshold and into the house. Sam pulled the door shut, and the president heard him descend the steps. He would be stationed outside in the darkness, invisible until he chose to reveal himself.

"What can I get you?" Sarah said from the kitchen. "I have a little bit of Scotch, some Budweiser—" He could hear bottles clinking. "Oh, and one bottle of cab, but it's not very good. Maybe we can give that to your friend." One of the guys, he knew, would be in there with her, standing unobtrusively in a corner. Right about now, he would shake his head, smiling politely.

"A glass of water would be fine," the president replied. She had hung up her coat on a wall rack made from deer antlers and hooves. He touched one of the antlers—smooth, cool bone—and took off his suit jacket. She stuck her head around the kitchen doorway, looking a little embarrassed. "This was my grandfather's house. He was a taxidermist."

"It's great," Bill said. "Completely authentic," he added, looking around. His head was still fuzzy. He blinked and wandered the periphery of the strange room, an amalgam of two very different generations. There were contemporary cream-colored sofas and chairs, but there was a familiar musty smell that would never be in a new home. He spied cardinals and blue jays in life-like poses on the windowsill. Antique jigsaws hung on the wall, as well as a mirror that said Irwin's Feed and Seed. He remembered the Coca Cola mirror in the house on East 13th Street, where they had moved with Roger; it had an image of a little girl and a white cat. He could picture his mother primping in front of it before Roger came home from work, her hands fluttery with anticipation about which Roger was actually going to show up—the one who grunted and ate supper in silence or the one who came home affectionate, unpredictable, and reeking of whiskey, the one who had aimed a gun at them both when Bill was five.

"Lock up your troubles in an airtight box," his mother had liked to say. She had stood in the doorway of his room on that night with the gun, and said it to him where he lay in bed, his eyes wide open and the covers drawn up to his neck. She came over and sat down next to him and stroked his hair and then she said it again and again. He loved it when she said those words. He loved to imagine his troubles inside the box, futilely scratching and howling like feral cats. He loved the satisfying click of the lock. Sometimes he imagined dropping the box into the ocean.

"Here you go," Sarah said, handing him a glass of ice water. She held a glass of the supposedly dreadful wine. She shrugged. "Somebody's got to drink it," she said.

"Thanks." He took a sip. He hadn't realized until that moment how dry his mouth was, how hot. He could feel the trail of the cold water in his throat.

"The photos are in here," Sarah turned on the light in the dining room. "The group that's ready to leave the darkroom, at least. They're a series."

He squinted, adjusting to the bright light. He felt a little dizzy and blinked to get his bearings. He walked up to the wall and began to study the dozens of framed black and white photos there, floor to ceiling, some poster-sized, and some tiny as matchbooks. At first, he saw only soft curvy patterns, like the hem of a skirt, or the edge of the sea. But then his eyes snapped into focus. What he was seeing was dozens of flared wings, a set within nearly every photo.

He looked closely at what was in front of him. This one was a sparrow on the windshield of a car, its wings spread slightly and its beak open, some of its blood just visible on the glass. The next one was a duck in a tall patch of weeds, its body stiff and straight and long. Then he saw a mourning dove on the asphalt, its neck at a strange angle and its eyes closed so peacefully, little half circles that children drew to indicate sleep.

He moved along the wall, taking in what the display offered. There were seagulls, chickadees, robins, grackles, and even a chicken. All of them dead. Many on the hoods or grills of cars. Others, the small ones, in someone's cupped hands. It was the quantity in such a small space that overwhelmed him. He felt hot, a little nauseated.

He pulled out one of the dining room chairs and sat down. "Boy, you're full of surprises," he said. He tried to train his eyes on Sarah's face, the motion behind those big dark eyes. No, this was no reporter. "How did you find them all?"

"It's not as hard as you would think. You just have to look out for them." She turned and pointed to a photo of a robin on its back in a wheelbarrow full of mulch. Its feet looked so delicate, like twigs. "This one, for example," she said. "Big Fred, the foreman at the lumberyard, called me up and said, 'Get over here. We got something for you.' Everyone in town knows what I'm up to. I get a call at least once a week."

"I had no idea birds had it so tough," he said, laughing.

"Yeah, well, I don't think it's just birds," she said, looking right at his eyes, but only for a second.

"You got me there," he said. They were both quiet for a moment.

She turned back to the robin. "This one. I think it flew into the side of the building during a storm. I don't know if you can see the little dent in its forehead. Right there. See?"

He stood up and looked closely. Sure enough, the bird was perfectly intact except for the side of its head, which was just slightly caved in. "Oh yeah," he said. "I see it."

"Normally, they huddle together in the trees during bad weather. Where could he have been going?" Her nose wrinkled and her eyes probed the president's face, as if he might actually be able to answer this question.

"They're very good. Compositionally and thematically. You've shown them?"

Sarah nodded. "Just at some community art shows and stuff. I almost got them into a big show at a gallery in Baltimore last month. It'll happen eventually. For now, I'm paying the rent with weddings."

"It's how you're keeping your dreams alive. Nothing wrong with that," he said, his tongue thick in his mouth. Was it possible that she'd spiked his champagne with something? No, Sam would've found anything before he put her in the limousine. It was just his meds. "If you want to do something, Sarah," he continued, "you just have to go for it. That's right. You're a lot like someone else I know," he said.

But then he wasn't sure. He had lost his wife long ago, well before he'd lost his mother. Had the other women come first or had he lost her first? Not a day went by that he didn't miss Hillary, the way she was long before they took the national stage, the dead-on impressions she used to do of their professors at Yale Law School, the way she would recite her latest haiku when they were in the bath together, the electric intelligence of her eyes and the way it warmed him inside, right through his gut. Now he mainly saw it when she was mad, when she was yelling at him. That moment earlier in the day, collaborating on the speech— that was the exception that proved the rule.

And none of the women he'd been with had even begun to fill that void. If he ever stopped wanting Hillary, the one thing in the world he couldn't have, would he stop wanting all of them? He reached out for Sarah's hand, the hand that had gotten him here in the first place. It was so smooth and young. He kissed her palm, still dry, then her wrist. He pulled her toward him.

Sarah hesitated, but then she smiled a little sadly. She touched his shoulder, and then she bent down and hugged him tightly, her hand on the back of his neck. "I feel like I know you, Mr. President," she said.

All of the girls said this to him, but normally it happened afterward, when they were lying next to him naked and breathless. When they said that, it was as if they pressed a button that caused the joy of the whole encounter to fly away from him. Me? he would wonder. Overweight, puffy-eyed me? But it wasn't like that with Sarah now. Why was that? Did he maybe feel the same about her—like she was familiar? Or more simply, that this place where she'd brought him felt like the home of his youth that no one really knew, the place no videographer or reporter had been able to get right?

That she was, in fact, a stranger, someone he'd met by chance and had, truth be told, just wanted to be with for the night, made him want to cry. A gulping sob lurked in his throat. He breathed deeply, smelling

Sarah's hair, like pineapple. He laughed a little. "I wish I knew you, really knew you," he said, not just to Sarah but to all of them, to his wife and his mother. Maybe it was luck—something impossible to box up, store, manipulate—that had brought them into his life at all. The thought that this might be true made him feel sick all over again. "You seem like such a very good woman, Sarah Heston."

He fumbled with his pager, signalling to Sam he was ready to go. Out on the street, as the president was about to get in the car, Sam put a hand on his shoulder. He leaned close and whispered in the president's ear. "Cold fish. Better luck next time," he said.

Sam's comment amused the president. "Thanks, Sam," he said, and then he went into a parody of his own 1992 campaign speech, complete with hand gesture. "I still believe in a place called Hope," he drawled. And with these words, the strange sensation he felt, which he could only just identify as doubt, the president's heart fluttered in the grill of his chest like it was made of birds' wings.

Indian Summer

The thick July breeze, which fluttered the bedskirt and the novel I'd left open on the night stand, carried the sound of crackling gravel into the room. I sat up on one elbow, looked out the second-floor window behind my head, and saw my cousin Raymond's Buick pulling down the long driveway. After he parked and got out, the car door echoing behind him in the early morning air, I watched him linger at the back door. For a minute, he looked stiff and pained, old enough to be my grandfather, not just my father. Then he stretched his back with a swift shoulder twist, and whispered to himself, maybe rehearsing, and I decided not to yell down like I wanted to.

I had been lying in bed, holding the faded old figurine of the girl and the lamb loosely in my fingers. It felt sturdy, like most of the things in my great-aunt Bunny's house. I had been thinking about what its original color might have been, about getting out of bed, about how my mom and stepdad Dale would be back from Maine in a few days. I wondered if three weeks of vacation meant they wouldn't walk around the house so obviously thinking about my still-born baby sister Madison anymore, or if maybe they would seem like different people altogether.

Raymond had been the closest thing to a companion I'd had over these three weeks. He would bring Taco Bell burritos in the afternoons, and the two of us would sit on the wrought iron lawn chairs and play War with a deck of cards and talk about things. But now, I judged from his dress pants and loafers, he was here to see Bunny on business. I took off my nightgown and put on my Old Dominion boxer shorts and yellow tank top, the same outfit I'd been wearing for most of my three weeks at the farm, and listened at the stairwell. In the front hallway Bunny and Raymond were whispering to each other, most likely because they thought I was asleep, not because they were keeping secrets, which neither of them could do even if they wanted to.

A half hour later, while Raymond and Bunny drank tea and talked in the kitchen, I sat cross-legged on the living-room floor and pretended to

Flann

read the personalities section of *The Washington Post*. Every few seconds, I looked out the window at the dirt road behind the farmhouse and waited for Bunny's summer farmhand, Jason Casey, to come in from the pasture to feed the goats.

"For Pete's sake, Raymond," Bunny said, her voice rising enough for me to hear, "I just thought those old people might like to eat some potato salad and meet folks. I'm not asking you to let them jump out of a plane." I could hear Bunny's chair slide back and the rustle of her pink slacks as she shifted, maybe to sit up straighter and cross her arms.

"A lot of my clients are medicated for serious health problems," Raymond said. "Plus, it'll be ninety-some degrees. An ambulance at the barbeque is a precautionary measure, nothing more." His voice cracked like it always did when he tried to sound business-like. He cleared his throat, as if, belatedly, to hurry the conversation along. "It's my job to think about things like this. Smoky Ordinary isn't a small town anymore. What if it gets out of hand? What if several hundred complete strangers show up? Have you thought about the insurance implications?"

Raymond had stopped by on his way to the Indian Summer Retirement Community, the nearest neighbor to Bunny's farm. As director, he had explained, he had to ensure that his clients would be safe if he let them come to Bunny's Barbeque Wing-Ding that afternoon. It was the biggest annual summer event in Smoky Ordinary, and Bunny invited pretty much everyone unless they had shown poor judgment at a previous Wing-Ding.

Bunny had specially invited the people from Indian Summer because, she said, the way they were always doddering onto her property proved that they were bored, bored like cows at a chess match. "I thought those old people might like to get out and enjoy themselves." Bunny was seventy-five herself. "I don't know how they can do that with an ambulance following them everywhere like death itself."

"Please," he said. His tone made me jerk up from the newspaper, like I'd been jabbed with a safety pin. He spoke in just the matter-of-fact way I had imagined Madison would when she was old enough to ride the coin-operated horse in front of the K-Mart. "Please," she would say, perfectly reasonable, and we would have to give her a couple of quarters. I'd revealed some daydream along those lines right before my mom and stepdad had left. It had become a fight, my mom yelling about "foolish thoughts that just weren't healthy."

Aunt Bunny was somebody who yelled a lot. She didn't normally compromise; it was more like her to shout and then throw something harmless, whatever was handy—a clothespin, a spare house key, a clip-on earring. But Raymond's wife and nine-year-old son had left him recently, and people tended to be careful with him, the way they were with Mom and Dale. People treated Raymond a little like he was elderly himself, though he was only thirty-eight, younger than my mother.

"You'll hardly notice the ambulance," he said. "And it'll give you so much peace of mind." Bunny kept quiet, which meant she was letting him win. I could picture the curt way she might be shaking her head.

The cuckoo clock on the wall over my head whirred then and the little bird popped through its doors eight times. I knelt on the couch across from where I had been sitting and pulled back the curtains and saw Jason Casey's black pickup truck chugging up the dirt road from the fields.

Raymond and Bunny came out of the kitchen then; she held a dish towel in her hands. "Looks like we're going to have the rescue squad at our little picnic," she said and wrinkled her nose; Raymond gave me a sly thumbs up. They stood side by side like children in a spelling bee, waiting, I knew, for my approval.

I had been arbitrating their debates about the old people for almost a month—about whether they should be allowed to eat chocolate or to swim in the pool or to take unsupervised showers. I had even been asked for my opinion about whether Bunny should be allowed to take her buggy over there and let the goats take Raymond's clients on rides around the heavily shrubbed and mulched grounds. After I sided with Raymond, Bunny had started treating me the way she had years ago—she made shortbread cookies for me that afternoon and spoke to me sweetly, like I might be a little retarded. It struck a nerve, because I knew I was different than before and that some people might think I was messed up. When my own aunt revealed that sort of confusion, switching from exaggerated consideration of my opinions to attempts to bribe me, I felt more alone than ever. And going to my old friends was out of the question. I never wanted to be with other people who were fifteen like I used to be when Madison was still around, still a possibility.

I calculated what I should say about the ambulance very carefully. "Hmmmm," I said, "interesting," and I looked out the window again.

Bunny and Raymond began to talk to each other, but I had stopped listening to their words. Jason got out of the truck. He wore Levi's and a pair of work boots. No shirt. He took off his Atlanta Braves baseball cap, ran his hand through his almost black hair, and put the cap back on. Jason had just graduated from my school, and I knew that he'd been

143

treasurer of Future Farmers of America because when I'd looked him up in the yearbook a few weeks earlier, it said so next to his name.

Jason was drinking water from a jug that'd been behind the seat. "Is it hot out yet?" I said, knowing the canopy of oak and pine trees around the house provided no relief past the front porch. The white sunlight bore down on the truck and the tool shed and the goat pen, which all lay just beyond the house like buoys that marked us off from the open sea of fields and pastures. I liked it out here on the farm. You could almost forget about the traffic and buzz of the DC suburbs, just a few miles away.

"I reckon," Bunny said. "On the news last night, twenty people died of heat stroke up in Philadelphia. We need to keep plenty of Cokes cold this afternoon. And we need to make sure the deacon doesn't drink himself silly under the blazing sun."

The deacon could take care of himself, I thought. He was the one who had sold off the left half of Our Redeemer Baptist Church to a medical center. Now there were two front doors. I pointed to the window. "He's out there."

Bunny gasped. "The deacon?"

"Jason Casey," I said and pressed my finger onto the warm window pane.

"He's the one you told me about," Raymond said. He smiled, an incongruous look pulling his ashen face tight. Raymond hadn't been looking too well since Eugenie left him and worse since he'd started living with a young breakfast waitress in an apartment in Brilliant, the next town. He had dark circles under his eyes, he'd put on weight, and someone fairly unskilled had let his pants out, stray threads sticking out where the old seams had been. "This guy might be just what the doctor ordered," he said, coming up behind me to stare out the window. "But you better be careful not to get carried away."

"Jason's never going to make it to the community college," Bunny said. "Don't get me wrong, I'm glad to have him around. But all he knows is cattle. Period. If he's really lucky, he can work out at the Toyota dealership with the rest of his family." She shuffled across the knotted wood floor and rubbed the coffee table with a corner of the dish towel, trying to remove a water ring on the glass.

I had been the one to leave the mark on the table. I had been sneaking back downstairs at night and eating Saltines with peanut butter and drinking milk and watching *CNN* and *The Weather Channel*. I felt most comfortable when no one could see me. I liked the idea of being so alone that no one could even picture me; I didn't want any evidence to give me away. Now, I wondered if Bunny had spotted the cracker crumbs between the couch cushions, too.

Jason Casey put his water jug back in the truck and shut the door. I had a strange desire to confide in him that conversations about hairstyles and movies made me angry when there were so many problems in the world like war and heartbreak and tornadoes. I let the curtain drop. "We should get to work," I said, pointing to the clock. "I wouldn't just go speak to him anyway," I concluded. "That would be weird."

Raymond stayed and helped us prepare for the party a while, probably to pay penance for the ambulance argument. He snatched Bunny's apron from a hook in the kitchen, put it around his neck, and tied it behind his light blue shirt, his fingers clumsy as if they didn't know each other. While Bunny took inventory in the cellar freezer of all the casseroles and pies we'd made ahead of time, I shredded carrots in the food processor in the kitchen. Raymond chopped cabbage on the whale-shaped cutting board, stopping every now and then to bite his cuticles.

I dumped the carrot shavings into a bowl. "So what do you think about Jason?" I asked.

"What do you think about him?" Raymond said. Turning the question around on me was just what the hospital-assigned counselor had done when she talked to us about Madison, about the way Madison had been suffocated by the umbilical cord.

I went to the fridge for the mayonnaise, soaking in the cold air until my knees got cold. "Don't do that," I said. "I want to know what you think."

Raymond shrugged. "All I can know for sure is what's in my own heart. When I first saw Frannie waiting tables at the IHOP," he said, "it was Flag Day, and a bunch of veterans had come in, swearing and playing grab-ass. First thing she did was spill a whole tray of orange juice on a guy in a Harley jacket. I knew right then how it would be. Sometimes, I want to throw my body between her and the world. Have I told you this story before?"

"Yes," I said, holding the bowl while Raymond scooped the cabbage into it. "Sounds intense."

As I measured out mayonnaise, Raymond salted the mixture, his silver watchband jingling. "What you need," Raymond said, "is someone to watch over you."

"I don't know about that," I said. "I don't like the idea of people needing each other. It's all sort of gross."

"Gross?" he laughed. "Well then why is it you're thinking about Jason Casey?" He took off his watch and set it on the black and white speckled counter top, and he rubbed his temples, his eyes closed, his lips in a slight sad smile. "Don't get mad at me for saying this, but I worry that you're afraid of people now." He seemed like he would say something more. A cardinal stirred in the bushes outside the window over the sink, and I pretended to study it, and then Raymond started mixing the coleslaw with a big wooden spoon. "That reminds me," he said. "I saw your friend Stacy at K-Mart last night. She asked about you."

"Oh yeah?" I said. "What did she say?"

"She wanted to know why you don't call her anymore."

I leaned against the counter, my arms crossed. "What'd you tell her?"

"I told her that I thought you needed your friends and that she shouldn't give up. I told her to look for you at the barbeque today."

"Oh God, Raymond," I said. "What'd you do that for? I don't want to talk to her."

"Why not?" he asked. "I still don't get it."

"I just don't," I told him. Stacy Neff had been my best friend. Before Madison died, we used to go roller-skating every Friday night at Roll-A-While, and Stacy still went sometimes with some other girls. She still called to invite me or just to talk, and she had even been calling me out at Bunny's. It bothered me. Sometimes I pretended not to be home. "I can't be this perfect teenager like everyone wants," I said.

"Hey," he said. "Don't worry. I want you to be as screwed up as the rest of us."

I smiled then in spite of myself. "Can I tell you something?" I asked.

"Shoot."

"It's really disgusting when you chew your fingernails over the food."

He pretended to gag and then grinned at me. "Thanks," he said. "I'll work on that one."

After Raymond left and Bunny set about dusting the bedrooms, I checked the list on Bunny's fridge. I chose to clip the hedges because this would take me outside, where I had a clear line of sight to the barns, way out in the pasture, where Jason Casey would probably be working.

My hair blew in the hot gust that met me on the back porch. The sweet smells of pine and crepe myrtle mingled with the musty odor of grasses, and I gasped for breath. I stopped for a minute, and something in the sweet outdoor smells and silence reminded me of the hospital. All three of us—Mom, Dale, and I—had gasped for breath, none of us able to protest, to say a word. We believed that, sure, Mom's labor was a little long and the baby was bound to be a little distressed, but these doctors knew what they were doing. We should have known better, I thought now. We helped each other not to do anything, to stay meek, not to shout, not to hold a scalpel to their noses and make them do a C-section.

I had a recurring dream where I found out that Madison wasn't really dead. Instead, I discovered each time, she'd been staying at Miss Eartha Demilo's house, our babysitter/fortuneteller neighbor at my real home in town, and I'd forgotten to pick her up. I always felt panicky, the way I did when I forgot my homework, and then relieved, like at the end of a scary movie. It was the best dream I ever had, though, because I could pretend things were different.

I pushed my hair out of my eyes and decided to see if I could sprint to the tool shed, where I needed to go for the hedge clippers, within a ten count. I swung my arms with each number as I dashed off the steps, the dry grass poking the bottoms of my bare feet. I burst out of the shade, the sun flashed, and I threw one arm up to block it and kept running, the shed squatting on the grass ahead like a hobo in a pointed hat. When I reached it, I slapped the whitewashed wood and rounded the corner toward the door. I stopped short when I saw the back of Jason Casey's truck just a few feet away and Jason himself over in the goat pen when he should have been long gone. I unlatched the door and slipped inside the shed, stepping onto the dirt floor. It was dark except for some spidery cracks of daylight in the ceiling and the spray of sun from the partially open door. I heard myself breathing and became frightened. The only time I'd ever spoken to Jason Casey was the first time I'd seen him, last month on the weekend of the funeral. Bunny had insisted on feeding us that Sunday night. And while we were inside, Hubert, the big goat, stole my algebra book through the car window, took it to his shelter, and ripped out the intro to fractions before Jason got the book away from him.

"My book," I'd said when he handed it back. I later changed the incident in my mind so that I'd said much wittier things, but I never changed the way he looked at me. I liked to play it over and over—the way he reached toward me with the book and beamed like someone who knows something important and good. He was the only person in my life who could smile like that just then. It didn't feel like disrespect at all, more like wisdom. It surprised me, and, for a minute, raised me up.

In the shed, I rummaged through the tool bin for the garden shears, comforted by the heft of Bunny's old metal instruments in there. When

Flann

I grasped the wooden handles of the shears firmly, I tugged them loose from the trowels, saws, tiny hoes, and stray horseshoes.

Peering out, I saw Jason slowly coming right toward me, toward the shed door. I coughed to announce my presence, sputtering as I came out and latched the door behind me.

"Hey. How's it going?" Jason said. I jumped as if he'd startled me and I put my hand on my heart. "Didn't mean to scare you," he said.

His tall form, tight and broad as a bale of hay, startled me up close and I leaned against the shed, catching my breath for real, my heart feeling like he truly had caught me off guard. "It's okay," I said.

He waved his hands in front of his bare chest, which in spite of its muscled ridges, looked vulnerable like chests of people I'd seen in medical reports on TV. "I'm sorry," he said and then he gazed at me, his mouth open a little. "You're Tanya McAllister."

"It's Tanya Sweeney. Dale McAllister is my stepfather." There was a pause. We stood about five feet apart. I couldn't decide whether to step closer because I didn't know if the conversation would continue or if it was pretty much finished. In any case, I was glad he didn't press me about my father. I didn't want to lie and hated to explain that he was a quarry worker from Petrie who'd split up with my mom when I was three. I never talked about how Mom and I had lived in Section Eight low-income housing until she met Dale at the post office, where she worked. I liked to focus on the part later, when I was eight, and we moved into Dale's house and he put a twin bed with a purple bedspread in the room that would be all mine.

"Dale and my dad know each other from the American Legion," Jason said to me. "Real sad thing about Dale's little girl." He shaded his eyes with his hand and leaned back to stare at the sky, like it might be disrespectful to look at me then.

It felt strange that he knew who I was and about my life, that he'd taken enough interest to remember, though he didn't seem to completely understand how our family fit together. I guessed I couldn't blame him for that. "What're you doing out here?" I asked, hoping he couldn't tell I knew his schedule.

"I decided to wash these goats before the barbeque. They'll be coming up to people and begging." He grinned as if he was proposing some mischief of his own.

"I'll help you."

He shook his head and turned and hoisted a hose from the back of his truck. "Well, if you want to."

148

"I want to," I said and tossed the hedge clippers to the ground. "Tell me what to do."

Jason hooked the long hose up to a new spigot at the corner of the shed—he'd laid the pipe from the line beside the house a few weeks before—and filled two buckets with soapy water. The goats paced in nervous circles in the corner of the pen.

Bunny kept goats because they chewed the grass short. Besides that, they didn't do much. But the big one, Hubert, did know enough to get that hangdog, tail-between-the-legs look when he'd get caught after sneaking into the house and sleeping on the guest bed upstairs.

Jason Casey spent more time with the goats than Bunny did—she thought half the reason to own them was that they didn't need much care. I watched him often through the window, talking and scratching their bellies, sometimes appearing to sing to them.

"You ready?" Jason said, squinting into the sun, and when I nodded, he turned on the faucet. I picked up the hose and pointed it at the goats, who clambered farther into the corner, beyond the pitiful stream in front of me. "Put your thumb over it," he said quietly. The water came out then in a thin, powerful stream that made a hollow sound on the goats' ribs. They stamped their feet and shivered their nubby tails, which made Jason laugh as he watched me work. When the goats were thoroughly soaked and their scraggly hair dripped water onto the grass, I dropped the hose and reached for one of the buckets. "You don't have to do that," Jason said, putting his hand on my arm. "They'll get you all muddy."

"But I want to," I said, glancing at his dark hand with its clipped fingernails and small white scars.

"Here. You can hold this brush for me. That would help a lot." Jason took hold of one of the goats in what looked like a wrestling move and began to scrub with the brush from the other bucket, which looked identical to the one I now held. I could still feel the place where his hand had been on my arm; it made the hairs stand up the way a caterpillar could when it dropped out of a tree onto my skin. Jason began what I learned was his routine with all the goats—he cleaned the ears, checked the eyes, teeth, and hooves; groomed all the burrs from the legs and belly. His lean fingers surprised me with their precision, almost like those of a seamstress, and with their tenderness when he would stroke the goats' boney chins. I leaned against the fence and ran my thumb over the coarse bristles of the scrub brush, and I realized that Jason Casey wasn't worried about me, about whether or not I'd get muddy. He just didn't trust anyone else with his goats.

I thought about how, at the hospital after Madison died, Dale and I had tried to check everything for flaws, as if we could make the grieving process that was about to begin just a little smoother by examining Mom's pillowcase, the yellowish liquid dripping down the tube, the elastic of her pajama sleeves. When Mom was awake, she snapped at us. "Cut it out!" she would say, her eyes big, and she'd run her hand through the dark roots of her short blonde hair. "Don't hover over me." I would go sit outside the room, sometimes picking up things the other new mothers on the ward had dropped or helping their toddlers to the water fountain or watching them wheel down the hall with their flowers and balloons. "I'm sorry," Mom would say to me later, after Dale had come and cried quietly into his hands by the vending machines or gone down to the parking lot and swung his baseball bat against the trunk of a pine tree.

I saw Jason's needless grooming and cleaning of the goats and heard the soothing way he spoke in their ears. I saw the worry, resigned and quiet, like my mother's for me when she would drop me off for school on her way to the post-baby hospital appointments. I could not think of him the way I had before. He was not the way he seemed from the window—simple and self-evident like a dog, a golden retriever. His dedication touched me, and at the same time seemed out of place, a little much.

"I'll take that brush now," he said, squatting on his heels, still scrubbing.

I waved it in front of him. "Why? It's just like the other one. You don't need it."

He looked back at me, surprised and maybe irritated. "What?" he said.

I stepped closer and shoved him with my index finger. He tipped over like a beetle. Then I did something even more strange: I lunged toward him, my hands at his shoulders and then his face, as if I could understand myself only by touching him, like I was a blind person who needed the knowledge sight would provide. And then—because I didn't know what else to do—I kissed him square on the lips. He gasped like he had asthma.

I jumped away and scrambled to my feet and dropped the brush in the bucket. "I have to go," I said without looking at him there, sprawled out on the dirt floor of the goat pen, and I ran inside.

Later, while The Lonesome Rangers, a country and western band, set up in the field out back, and the Quality Meats people rigged up the pre-roasted pig on the spit, in a daze I cleaned up and put on a denim mini-skirt, a collared blue shirt, and white tennis shoes. As I combed my hair into a ponytail, the phone rang and Bunny yelled up that my mother was on the phone. For a second, before my mother spoke, I thought she'd called because she knew what I'd done.

"We bought you a T-shirt and a necklace and earrings and some other things. Some surprises," she said. I could hear people arriving outside, digging for beer and Coke in the trash can full of ice. "I can't wait to see you," she said.

"When are you going to come get me?" I asked, trying to picture how our lives would be when they returned, how dinner would be, who'd talk and where we'd sit.

"As soon as we get home," she said. I could hear Dale speaking in the background then. "Dale sends his love. He's been talking about you non-stop. Tell us how you are."

I felt like I'd plunged into ice water myself. "Well," I said, "I'm wondering if the sight of each other will make us all feel bad."

She was silent for a moment. "Honey," she said almost as a question, "you know I love you."

"Yes," I said. "I know." And I let her go on talking for a while. She sounded relieved.

When I got off the phone and finally got back outside, the band had started playing "Blue Moon of Kentucky" and three people danced—my history teacher Mr. Harrison danced the two-step with his new wife, and Elliot Simms, a gifted boy a year younger than me who sometimes followed girls into the restroom, flailed wildly by himself. Over by the pig, a whole group of men, including the mayor, stood around in chino and Bermuda shorts, drinking beer and arguing about the Virginia Tech football team.

While a group of women hovered around the food tables arranging plastic forks and baskets of chips, Bunny hustled with trays of carrot sticks, cheese, and pickles, and with bowls of ambrosia, macaroni, and olive salad, kicking the screen door open and letting it slam shut behind her. Hope and Joy Mullins, popular twins from school, stood over by the goat pen laughing and flirting with Jason Casey, who had put on a black T-shirt with a car on the front of it. He waved at me when I looked, and the two girls stopped laughing. I waved back, but I felt

151

guilty, like we knew secrets about each other now, secrets that made me want to disappear into the crowd so he couldn't see me anymore.

The group dancing grew, and more people were coming all the time—I could hear the tires of one car after another crunching the gravel on the long driveway in front of the house. A briefly sounded siren echoed over the house and twisted through the swarms of gnats and little white flies in the humid air, as the rescue squad and hook and ladder approached, drove up on the grass to pass the cars and parked next to the band. The Indian Summer Retirement Community Excursions Bus, with my cousin Raymond at the wheel, followed close behind. Medics and firefighters in blue shorts and polo shirts helped the old people—many of whom wore "Senior Fun Bunch" T-shirts—off the bus. Raymond massaged some men's shoulders like they were boxers and he offered his arm to a petite lady wearing red lipstick. He gathered his group and spoke to all of them excitedly about remembering any special diets and about wearing sunblock, about turning down their hearing aids near the speakers and keeping tabs on their section leaders, mostly youngish women with permed hair whom he made raise their hands before everyone took off. Then, he asked the one person in a wheelchair, Mrs. Fitch, what she'd like to do first and he wheeled her into the crowd.

As for me, I helped some women with the food for a while and then I watched the band and tried to figure out where I'd seen the singer before finally recognizing him as a cashier from Biscuitville. I wandered back to the food and ate two deviled eggs and, feeling comfortably invisible in the crowd, reached for a third, even though there were only a few left on the Chinette paper plate. It was then that I saw Stacy standing alone at the other end of the table, rocking on her heels, smiling to the music like she was the homecoming queen.

I walked over and touched her shoulder. "Hi," I said.

She tried to hide her surprise—not that I was there, but that I'd approached her. "We missed you at the roller rink last night," she said. "Hank Henderson flipped over the railing and chipped a tooth."

This was the kind of thing, a few months back, we'd have stayed up late laughing about. But lately, I hadn't been able to stand listening to Stacy, or even looking at her. There was nothing wrong with her blonde hair or her pink lips and matching pink shirt. I knew that she liked me and didn't understand the way I acted. It didn't matter. She got under my skin. Nothing had changed at her house like it had at mine, and her problems seemed so small, and no one ever asked questions about how she fit into her own family. I saw her as dense sometimes, and it made me want to say things that could hurt her or make her go away. "It's not very nice to laugh about someone chipping a tooth," I said.

"Oh, he was all right," she said. "I think he sort of liked the looks of it."

I looked away. An old man, one of Raymond's, was spraying Easy Cheese right into his mouth like a kid.

Stacy crossed her arms; she stuck out her bottom lip and blew her bangs off her forehead. "Hope Mullins told me that Jason Casey really likes you," she said. "He's hanging around over there, trying to get up the nerve to talk to you." I looked where she pointed, but I didn't see anything except some women from the Garden Club line dancing. Stacy looked at me then in such a decent, honest sort of way, sort of like a Girl Scout on a poster, that I felt bad.

"You've always got the good dirt," I said, and thought about hugging her, but then also, I didn't want to.

She sipped from her can of Pepsi, laughing. "That's true." Peter Gregg, the State Farm Insurance representative, was leaning over the coconut bars to make a pitch to Bunny, who waved him away like a noisy insect. "Want me to look for Jason with you?" Stacy said.

"No," I told her. "I should help Bunny. There's a lot still to do."

"I could help you," Stacy said, "if you want."

"That's all right."

"Will you call me tomorrow?"

"Maybe," I told her. "I'll try." I backed away, thinking that I could be telling the truth.

I had already lost Bunny and so I began to snake my way to the house. Intermittently visible through the crowd, I could see Raymond lounging on the back steps with an Old Milwaukee. The hot breath of chattering mouths and the sweet fleshy smell of the pig and the busy shifting and pawing of dozens and dozens of shoes were overwhelming.

When I got to the edge of the crowd, I nearly tripped over Jason Casey, who was on the ground wrestling with a big brown dog, two guys cheering him on. "Hey," one of them said to Jason. "Hey!"

Jason looked at his friend, who glanced at me. Jason looked up at me then with the same curiosity he'd had earlier, and the dog continued to tug at the collar of his shirt. "We're going to get a brew," his other friend said, and the two of them slipped into the crowd, pointing to some girls who danced on top of the speakers.

Jason hopped to his feet and brushed himself off, the dog nipping at his wrists. "Knock it off," he said.

"This your dog?" I said, giving it a firm pat.

"Yeah," he said. "This is Jimmy. We were just messing around."

I inspected Jimmy—he was some kind of retriever with green, human-looking eyes. He licked my hand, and I laughed. I turned my attention to Jason, noticing a cowlick in the front of his dark hair, one I'd never seen because I'd never seen his hair freshly washed and combed, his skin powder dry. "I feel like I should say I'm sorry about earlier," I said, embarrassed, wondering if I'd have done the same thing to this clean, somehow smaller boy. But then he beamed, staring me full in the eye.

"You surprised me," he said.

"I don't know what happened," I said. My hands waved, trying to grasp more explanation. Finally, I let my arms drop. The band struck up their own personalized version of "The Old Rugged Cross" with a dulcimer and a steel guitar. Far in the distance, several turkey vultures circled in the clear blue sky over the road, probably attracted to something run over by one of Bunny's guests, a squirrel, maybe, or a snake. "I got scared," I said. "I'm not really myself right now."

"I wish we could start over," Jason said. "Because I'd like to ask you to go out with me sometime, to a movie or something."

"I don't know," I said, my face getting hot.

He stuffed his hands in his front pockets. "What would stop you?"

"Everything," I told him. I felt like my voice would break, and I couldn't say more. The dog threw himself at my feet then; his stomach looked more pink and tender than I thought it would. To keep from crying, I knelt down and rubbed it and his back leg pedaled out of control. The leg made me both happy and sad.

Jason was watching me. His face looked knit the way the goats' faces did when they sat on the front porch during a storm. "Are you still scared?" he said. "Is it me?"

"No. I think I do it to myself," I said. I closed my hand around the dog's paw and felt the knuckles and toenails, perfect like the clasp on a change purse. It took my wrist between its teeth, but gently, as if we were old friends. I had a strange feeling of relief. "Okay," I said.

Jason offered his hand when I started to get up. "When do you want to go?" he said.

"Next week," I told him. "But I'll be at home then. On Cottonwood Street." I pictured him strolling up our small front walk, his pleasant relaxed face like a glimpse of the cornflower blue sky over the goat pen.

When I got to the back porch, I turned around to look at Jason just as he threw a stick for the dog with a loose, sidearm motion. Jimmy retrieved the stick, then dropped it, and trotted circles around Hubert, who was gobbling potato salad off the fire chief's plate while the man's head was turned. Jason laughed, and that made me smile.

"What are you doing?" Raymond asked me, but before I got the words out, he said, "Sit yourself down right here," and he patted the concrete between Bunny and himself. Wedged between the iron railings, the space they created was pitiful, not bigger than my hand, and I squirmed in happily anyway. As I got settled, Raymond's stale, pungent beer breath wafted on the weak breeze. I waved my hand in front of my nose and made a face.

"I know," Bunny said. "Mr. Responsible." She rolled her eyes. "He'll be the one in that ambulance before the day's done."

"Hey," he said. "I put Judy in charge." He rested his beer on his knee and leaned forward to look at Bunny. "This is a good time. I thought you'd be happy I decided to enjoy it."

"That's all I wanted was for people to have fun." She lurched toward Raymond, squishing my arm. "Everyone."

"I have people to care for."

"Let's not think about it for a while," I said. "It's too much."

Bunny flicked Raymond's arm. "Fine with me," she said. I looked across the field that lay beyond the party and at the long shadows stretching across it like blindfolds. I could see Jason now lingering at the edge of the crowd, using his pocket knife to fix a man's arm brace. Hubert was vomiting into the bushes while the other goats scavenged among the hoards of party-goers.

Raymond finished off his beer and flexed the flimsy aluminum with his fingers. "Those goats are going to hurt someone or keel over, one," he started in, and they began to argue again.

The bickering didn't bother me now. I would only see the sun set, peeping over these particular trees, for three more days this summer. The crowd would be thinning out soon. Raymond would be going home to a young woman he barely knew, and maybe that would work out for them. Mom, Dale, and I would be learning to live together again.

I rubbed my hand on Raymond's back, which, under the broad girth, was spiny and fragile as a seashell. He twisted the tab off his beer can and dropped it inside, where it made a hollow clink—a faint call that was satisfying only because it marked a stop, if just a small one.

The Serena McDonald Kennedy Award

Serena McDonald Kennedy

Serena McDonald Kennedy was born in 1850 on the fourth of July. She was the fifth of seven daughters and the ninth of 12 children, of James and Serena Swain McDonald in Thomas County, Georgia. She was descended from Alexander McDonald, a Scottish Highlander, who fought with General James Oglethorpe at the Battle of Bloody Marsh, which saved Florida from the Spanish. His son was our Revolutionary hero.

Her father and mother, after marriage, settled on a farm between the McDonald and Swain plantations, later occupying the Reese plantation and finally the Swain plantation where they lived until their deaths. A town grew up around their home site named McDonald, Georgia, now known as Pavo, making James one of the first real estate developers of the area.

Serena, although far down the list of girls, had her mother's name, one, it was said, that fit her personality. Only a few years after her birth, her father would go to war as a Lieutenant-Colonel in the Confederacy, and she would lose a brother in the War Between the States. We have in our possession a long letter written in beautiful Spencerian script from her brother, Kenneth, a Captain, on April 20, 1863 (when she was 13 and he was 23), from "near Fredricksburg, Virgina." He wrote of the beauty* of Spring in Virginia, and as a postscript, he said: "You will excuse this miserable bad written thing of a letter; for God's sake don't show it." Only two weeks later, he was wounded at Chancellorsville and died three weeks later.

Serena was 30 years old before McDonald, Georgia, became Pavo, because of a conflict with the larger town named McDonough. At that time, a Mr. Peacock was Postmaster, and wanted the town to have his name, so in forwarding a group of names for selection to the U.S. Postal Service, he included Pavo (Latin for "peacock") and was the one chosen.

At 35, Serena was what was then generally called "an old maid," who came to the community of Enon in Thomas County as a school teacher. There she met and married John Thomas Kennedy, ten years her junior. Tom, as he was called, had lost a young wife and child in childbirth, and he and Serena began a life together that lasted for 40 years, until Serena died at the age of 75. Tom died 10 years later. They were the parents of four children, the second of whom was my father, Archibald Randolph Kennedy.

My grandmother was a great believer in education, and to our ultimate benefit, she saw that my father went to prep school and college, unusual in the rural area in which our family lived. His education influenced our family in many ways, and I attribute my love of literature to that heritage.

Although Serena died before I was born, my mother, Adeline Kennedy, was so devoted to her mother-in-law that she quoted her often and patterned our development after what she learned from her mother-in-law. My sister, Martha Stephenson, my brother, William Kennedy, and I are her only grandchildren living today. It is a great honor for us to have the Serena McDonald Kennedy Award named for her.

Barbara Kennedy Passmore

"The weather has turned warm and pleasant at last. The cold icy blast of winter has past and all nature looks revived. The sufferings of a cold hard winter seem to have been all forgotten and a few warm days have induced the trees to put forth their Buds and Blossoms. Everything seems to be in a high state of pleasure and glee. Everything is beautiful and harmonious. It's a bright Sabbath morning..."

–Kenneth McDonald

Former Winners of the
Serena McDonald Kennedy Fiction Award